REIGNITED

Agents of Ensenada, Book Three

Tess Summers
Seasons Press LLC

Originally published: 2019 with the subtitle Ensenada Heat

Republished: 2020 with the new subtitle Agents of Ensenada

Published by Seasons Press LLC.

ISBN: 978-1-966869-90-0

Edited by Maggie Ryan.

Cover by OliviaProDesign.

This is a work of fiction. The characters, incidents and dialogues in this book are of the author's imagination and are not to be construed as real. Any resemblance to actual events or persons, living or dead, is completely coincidental.

This book is for mature readers. It contains sexually explicit scenes and graphic language that may be considered offensive by some.

All sexually active characters in this work are eighteen years of age or older.

Reignited

He's known as the CIA's top mercenary fixer. But he can't fix this.

Jacob Smith

Seven years.

Seven long miserable years since he'd ripped his heart from his chest and left it on her doorstep when he walked away from her. But, he'd had no choice.

At least, he'd thought he hadn't. He was too entrenched in the CIA's underground world to safely ever have a wife and family.

But now, after turning his CIA dealings into a *very* lucrative mercenary career, here he was, about to embark on a ten-day cruise with his cabin next to hers, not by coincidence—although she didn't know it yet.

He wasn't known as a 'fixer' for nothing. Maybe it was time to try to fix his broken heart, and hers—if she'd let him. And that was a big *if*, given how he'd shattered hers so long ago.

Acknowledgements

The Tucson Hotties, Renee Rose and Misty Malloy—your friendship is priceless; my soul always feels lighter after hanging out with you two. I appreciate all your insights with this book and for helping me get unstuck. "Remember that time in San Diego when..."

Maggie Ryan—I'm so grateful that Renee recommended you. Thank you for everything you did to make this book better.

OliviaProDesigns—another amazing cover.

Janece Ellers—you are so fucking awesome. I love you. I appreciate you being available to read *every* book.

JM—I can't thank you enough for your feedback—from the beginning. I should have listened to you about Travis... lesson learned. I'll never doubt you again.

My mom, aunties, grandma, and cousins—you're the best tribe a girl could ask for. "Don't mess with my discount!!"

My dear readers—your support and encouragement humbles me every day. Thank you for letting me keep sharing my stories with you.

Last, but not least, Mr. Summers—thank you for always being there and holding everything together when it's ready to fall apart. You are the rock of our family, and I'm eternally grateful that you wanted to marry *me*. I love you.

Table of Contents

REIGNITED

Agents of Ensenada, Book Three

Chapter One

Taren Fairchild

She held her breath as she handed the young man in the white uniform her boarding pass. Even though the cruise line had assured her everything was paid for when she'd called directly two weeks ago, she was still nervous, wondering if they were going to let her on the ship. The tickets had shown up via courier the day after her divorce, and she had no idea who bought her the vacation—the typed note in the envelope simply said: *You deserve it. Enjoy.*

"Welcome aboard, Ms. Fairchild," the man said with a hospitality-perfected smile as he handed her boarding pass back to her. She let out a sigh of relief and smiled back, only hers was genuine. It felt weird to be referred to by her maiden name, but also liberating, and now that she was being allowed on board, she was filled with gratitude toward her mystery benefactor that she hadn't allowed herself to feel until just then.

Taren crossed the carpeted threshold into a circular atrium surrounded by six floors of decks. There were two glass elevators and a big bar in the middle of the sunken room with two strapping bartenders in blue Hawaiian shirts and white pants. She'd definitely be stopping by there after she found her stateroom.

"Excuse me, darlin'," a handsome middle-aged man said as he stepped in front of her on his way to the bar. His Cajun accent made her observe him carefully as he ordered his drink. When she'd asked the cruise line who purchased the tickets, the only thing the representative could tell her was they were bought through a travel agency out of New Orleans that catered to patrons worldwide.

Ah, New Orleans. Once her favorite city in the whole world—where she'd gone to college and had her first taste of independence. It was also where she'd met the love of her life. The one she was sure was going to ask her to marry him, only to dump her instead. Talk about being blindsided.

Jacob ending things without warning had left her devastated for years, unable to trust her judgment—which is probably how she'd eventually ended up married to David Graham. He'd made sure to do all the thinking for her.

Not anymore.

Taren looked up at the light coming in through the glass ceiling and smiled as she took a deep breath. *To my new life. To having independence again.*

****

Her steps were light as she made her way to her stateroom. A blond man with sunglasses on his head, dressed like he was a throwback from *Miami Vice* in an aqua t-shirt, pink blazer pushed up to his elbows, white pants and white shoes gave her a crooked smile—blatantly checking her out as he passed her in the hall.

Maybe I'll even get laid on this trip. Not with the Don Johnson wannabe—obviously—but she was sure there were plenty of single men on the ship. It'd been a long time since she'd had satisfying sex.

An older man in a white uniform greeted her just as she found her room number and slid her key card in the slot.

"Hello, Taren, welcome. I'm your steward, Manuel. Let me know if you need anything."

"How do you know my name?" she asked with surprise.

"It's the crew's job to know all our guests' names."

Impressive.

"Thank you, Manuel. I will."

She tugged her suitcase over the threshold and stepped inside, and after getting a glimpse of her cabin, immediately stepped back out.

"Manuel?"

He quickly turned around at the sound of her voice.

"Is there a problem, Taren?"

"Um, I think this is the wrong room."

She handed him her boarding pass, which he dutifully took and compared the number on the paper to the number on the door.

"This appears to be correct. Is there something wrong?"

"It's a suite."

He nodded in confusion—obviously not understanding what her problem was.

"I, uh, guess I didn't realize I was in a suite."

Manuel smiled at her. "Let me know if you need anything."

Walking back in, she pushed her suitcase further into the room while surveying her surroundings. *Who on earth bought me this cruise?*

That was the question she pondered the entire time she unpacked, and she was even more confused when Manuel delivered a bottle of her favorite white wine along with a single glass and a card that read, *Enjoy your vacation.*

"Would you like me to set this on the balcony? You might enjoy it while we leave port."

"That would be lovely. Thank you."

Taren stood to the side as he set the wine bucket on the small table outside the sliding door. Whoever her benefactor was, he or she or they, had great taste.

"What time do we leave?" she asked when he came back inside.

The steward glanced at his watch. "In two hours."

Following Manuel out the door into the hall, she said as she closed the door behind her, "I think I'm going to go to the lido deck and look around."

He replied with his usual mantra, "Let me know if you need anything."

****

Jacob Smith

He'd always considered himself a patient man—hell, he'd been keeping an eye on Taren for almost a year without having any contact. But the next few hours until they left the dock were going to kill him with anticipation.

Jacob had been content with biding his time until seven months ago, when the photos on his desk showed the dark circles under her blue eyes filled with sadness and tears when she thought no one was looking. Only then did he intervene.

The guilt that she had ended up with someone like Graham weighed heavily on him. He'd thought he had done the right thing by leaving her so she could find someone who would make her happy and keep her safe. His friend Mason's words on his jet one night haunted him until he took action.

Just because she moved on doesn't mean he's the better man for her. I guarantee no one could love Reagan better than me.

There wasn't a doubt in his mind that anyone would love Taren more than he did—it was the *better man* part that had initially given him pause. The better man would be able to guarantee her safety.

He was nervous about how she was going to react at seeing him. He couldn't remember the last time he'd been nervous. Maybe the last time he'd been with her and knew he was going to end things.

The bottle of wine he'd had delivered was supposed to ensure that she was on the balcony when they left the dock, but she seemed to be enjoying cocktails on the lido deck with a group of singles her age—dancing and waving at people on shore as they sailed away. One guy seemed to have taken a special interest in her and had positioned himself next to her at both the railing and on the dance floor. Taren wasn't exactly pushing him away, either.

Jacob hadn't taken into consideration she might hook up with someone else.

Fuck.

He sighed. This wasn't how he'd planned on revealing himself. He'd had visions of her being on her balcony, and he would be on his next door, and she'd see him—maybe let out a little gasp, then they'd proceed to talk. She on her balcony, Jacob on his. It seemed the most nonthreatening, in case she hated him. She'd have her own space to process his presence. Approaching her on deck, especially with Romeo next to her who appeared both testosterone and alcohol fueled, could backfire badly. But, watching the guy put his arm around her shoulder, he didn't have a choice.

Here goes everything.

Chapter Two

Taren

She really needed this guy to back off. Standing at the railing, he'd introduced himself as Peter as they left port and then attached himself to her side when she smiled and told him her name in return.

"I'm going to go to the bar. I'll talk to you later," she said with a polite smile as she ducked under his arm going around her shoulder.

"I'll go with you."

Taren almost said she was going back to her cabin instead, but didn't want to risk him following her and knowing which stateroom was hers. With a sigh, she resigned herself to escaping to the ladies' room once they reached the bar.

When she turned around, she came face-to-face with a ghost from her past, and it made her knees feel weak. How was it even possible he was standing in front of her? On a cruise ship out of San Diego of all places?

"Jake?" she whispered in wonderment.

Funny, he didn't seem surprised to see her.

"Hey, Tink."

From the first day they'd met, he'd called her Tinkerbell. He'd said she looked like she was sprinkling fairy dust on the campus mall that afternoon so long ago when he approached her on the grass at Tulane. It was the cheesiest pickup line she'd ever heard—and it worked. Or maybe it was his twinkling green eyes and high cheekbones.

He looked older now. Wiser. There was greying around his temples in his brown hair and lines around his eyes as he smiled cautiously at her, like he was unsure if she'd be happy to see him.

Peter put his hand on her elbow, and Jacob's eyes flashed. Time for her to take advantage of the long lost love of her life's appearance.

She threw her arms around her former lover's neck.

"Honey! There you are! Where were you?"

His smile was wicked as he slid his hands around her back and pulled her against him, and she realized she was in trouble. Jacob Smith had never been one to pass up an opportunity when it presented itself to him. Especially not when it was served up on a silver platter like she'd just done.

"I've been looking for you," he said, and then lowered his mouth onto hers.

That did the trick, because Peter slunk off, but that didn't make Jacob let up on the kiss.

The taste of his lips was soft and familiar, as was his scent, and she was taken back to a time when she was happy. Deliriously happy. She'd forgotten how wonderful he used to make her feel.

Tears welled up behind her closed eyelids, and she slipped her hands down his chest to fist his shirt in her grip while abruptly breaking the kiss.

"Tink..." he murmured against her lips.

"Why... Why did you leave me?" The words were out of her mouth with a small sob before she could stop them. *I haven't seen him in seven years, and I open with that?*

"I'm so sorry, baby." He tenderly kissed her wet eyelids, with one arm still wrapped around her, whispering, "So. Sorry," in between each kiss while he stroked her hair with his other hand.

She didn't forgive him—not by a long shot, but god, she loved how she felt right now as he held her. It was like going back to a time when she'd been happy and carefree. Her only care in the world was getting through finals and when she'd see Jacob next. They usually didn't get out of bed for the first forty-eight hours when he came into town. The last time she'd had really good sex had been with Jake. The man could do things to her body that no one had ever done. The orgasms he'd wring out of her would leave her comatose. Taren could stand to be in a sex stupor tonight—she *needed* it. She'd worry about the ramifications tomorrow.

The bon voyage piña coladas she'd imbibed had lowered her inhibitions and upped her libido, and she subtly ground her hips into his hard cock pressed against her.

Grabbing Jacob by the hand, she said with a coy smile, "Your cabin or mine?"

His voice was husky when he answered, "Yours."

"Follow me, sailor."

****

Jacob

He hadn't planned on sleeping with Taren right away. Not even close. They'd waited over a month to have sex when they'd started dating ten years ago, and that was with him flying into New Orleans every week for a three-day weekend and spending nearly every second with her—even tortuously sleeping in the same hotel room.

He'd assumed he'd have to grovel and woo her before getting into her bed again, show her that she could count on him—he wasn't going anywhere. Holding her soft hand as they quietly took the stairs to the deck where their cabins were located, all that seemed out the window, and he wasn't sure how he felt about it.

When she'd first invited him to her cabin, he had been all for it, needing to feel her naked body against his; the sooner, the better—or so he'd thought. But as they walked the hallways, he was becoming less sure. It felt like they should talk first—hash things out before sleeping together again.

"How are you here, Jake? How is this even possible?" she quietly asked as they made their way down the long corridor.

Jake. No one but his mom and Taren were allowed to call him that. He'd missed hearing it from her.

"I heard you were going to be here."

That caused her to stop dead in her tracks.

"*You,*" she hissed in accusation. "*You* bought me this cruise. How did you—" She paused as though at a loss for words, then shook her head, and tried again, unsuccessfully. "Why would you—"

She was obviously not happy with the realization that her ex-boyfriend was her vacation benefactor and tried to pull her hand away. Jacob tugged her against his chest instead, holding her tight so she had no choice but to listen as he pleaded his case.

"I needed to see you, Tink. Spend time with you," he murmured against her earlobe.

Taren refused to look at him, instead kept her eyes glued on the two-tone wall in front of her.

"And you couldn't have done that in Houston? How did you even know where I was?"

"I made some calls, did a little online digging. You weren't hard to find, little one."

She was scowling when she finally looked at him, obviously not a believer. She'd always known him better than anyone.

"And you just happened to be doing your research as I was getting divorced?"

Stepping back, Jacob released his hold and moved his hand to the small of her back, urging her forward. "Let's go to your cabin, and I'll explain..."

She pursed her lips and narrowed her eyes as she crossed her arms over her chest—not budging. There's that sass he loved; it was good to see the fire back in her eyes, even if her ire was with him.

He bent his knees so he was eye level with her and gave her his best puppy dog look—his hand still at her back. "Tink, come on. Please?"

Her face softened and she uncrossed her arms as she started walking again.

"Damn you, Jake. You always knew how to play me like a fiddle."

Jacob tugged on her arm so she would stop and face him.

"I never played you Taren—not then, and not now. I was out of my mind in love with you, and I still am. If you'll just hear me out..."

She stared at him with her mouth open, but nothing was coming out, like she was at a loss for words.

"Let's talk in your cabin, Tink," he suggested again.

She nodded in answer and started walking once more; a sense of relief coming over him that she was letting him take her to her room.

Chapter Three

Jacob

"This is just sex, Jake. It doesn't mean *anything*," she said as she reached behind her back and pulled the zipper of her dress down.

"Maybe we should talk first…"

He watched from his seat on her couch, captivated, as she slipped her arms out and let the material drop to the floor.

"I don't want to talk."

She'd gotten curvier since they were last together—and sexier, if that were possible. Her tits were fuller, hips wider, but she still had the strawberry birthmark just above her bikini line. The one he had loved to kiss.

Wearing nothing now but her white lace bra and panties, she boldly stepped closer.

"I mean it. No expectations of getting back together."

There was no way in hell he was agreeing to that. It was a hell of a lot more than sex, and he absolutely expected to get back together—it was all he'd thought about for the last seven months.

"God, you're beautiful," was his raspy reply as he stood and covered the remaining distance between them; the backs of his fingertips softly traced the exposed skin of her tits along the outline of her bra. A smile formed on his lips when her skin broke out in goosebumps, and she shivered at his touch. "So. Fucking. Beautiful. But, I really want to explain..."

She cut him off mid-sentence when she dropped her bra and pushed her bare tits against him. He bit back a groan. They needed to clear the air before they did this, but she was just too damn tempting.

She began to fondle his erection over his pants, and Jacob dipped his hand in her panties, watching her face for her reaction when he found her drenched and began to smear her juices around her clit.

"You're already wet, Tink."

She simply nodded, pulling her lower lip between her teeth as she closed her eyes and pushed against his hand.

He plunged one finger inside her and began to fuck her slowly, his thumb moving circles around her clit while never taking his eyes off her face.

"Do you need to be fucked, baby?" he growled as he pushed his middle finger deeper inside her.

Damn, she is tight. When was the last time she'd been fucked?

The material from her panties was impeding his movement, and he tugged on the lacy sides with his free hand until they were at her ankles, where she dutifully stepped out of them.

"Get on the bed."

She did exactly as he instructed, and he stood at the foot of the bed admiring her.

"Spread your legs for me. Let me see your pussy."

Again, she did as she was told. He had always loved her submission, in addition to her fire. It felt like a gift that she gave only to him. Considering he'd taken her virginity, at the time, it was. But even now, as she obeyed his commands, it felt special. He needed to remind her of what they once had.

"Jake..." She sat up and reached for his waistband, and he promptly pressed on her shoulder before tapping her inner thigh authoritatively.

"Keep your legs spread."

"It's just sex," she whispered—almost as if to remind herself, while she complied with his demands.

He swiped his tongue straight up her slit, causing her to jump, then swirled it around her clit. She tasted exactly like he'd remembered.

When she let out a whimper, it made him feel just cocky enough to disagree with her.

"No, Tink. It's so much more than that." He slid a finger back inside her pussy to fuck her while his tongue continued exploring her folds.

She didn't argue, which emboldened him.

"You're mine, little one."

"Hmph."

Jacob felt her response as she heaved the syllable from her chest more than he heard it. He needed her to agree with him. Fortunately, he had known how to play her body like an upright bass from the beginning. The way she was responding to him proved he hadn't forgotten. Maybe this was how he got through to her.

He switched his tongue and fingers so he was now polishing her clit with his hand and fucking her with his mouth.

When he felt her body begin to clench, he murmured against her pussy, "That's it, baby. Come on my tongue."

Taren shuddered underneath him, and he gently pressed on her stomach to keep her from writhing out of his control as he continued his attention to her pussy while she rode out her orgasm.

"Jake, please..." she gasped and pushed his head away from in between her legs.

He lifted his head with a smile, knowing her juices were smeared all over his face, and crawled up her body—still fully clothed with his cock pressing against his zipper. His intention had been to kiss her neck, but he got sidetracked by her luscious tits along the way.

His left hand gently squeezed the flesh on her right boob while his tongue and teeth became reacquainted with her left nipple. Her pert pebbled tips were at full attention for him.

"Mmm, good girl. So responsive," he moaned against her skin. In turn, she raised her hips to grind against his cock.

"Please fuck me," she whispered. "I need to feel you inside me."

Shit. He hadn't been expecting this when he left his cabin. This might be the perfect opportunity to slow things down.

"I don't have anything with me."

"I'm on the pill—and I'm clean. I promise. I got tested when I found out my husband was cheating on me."

"*Ex*-husband," he corrected. The way she was looking at him made him powerless. He needed to be inside her just as much. So, he added, "I'm clean, too, baby." He'd gotten tested last year when being with her again became a real possibility.

Jacob stripped out of his clothes in record time and resumed his attention to her tits, all the while she tried to maneuver her hips so his cock was between her legs.

He raised his head and smiled at her.

"Impatient, are we?"

As badly as he wanted to fuck her, he also wanted to savor this moment. It'd been too long since he had this woman underneath him. When he did fuck her, he wasn't going to last long, and he knew it.

She put her hands around his face and drew his mouth to hers, which surprised him. She never used to want to kiss him after he ate her pussy.

As their tongues tangled, he thought back to the hours they would spend just making out and realized he hadn't really kissed another woman since her. It was too intimate. Sure, he'd fucked plenty, but not since Tink had it meant something other than a way to carnal gratification. He wasn't a selfish lover—he always made sure his partners left satisfied. But, he also always made sure she—or they—*left*. He was looking forward to holding his little sprite in his arms all night long, and making love to her over and over again.

Because, it was going to be making love—whether she wanted to admit it or not.

He could feel the heat from her arousal, and putting his weight on his forearms, looked into her eyes as he entered her, letting her get used to his size before pressing all the way inside. When he was fully seated, they moaned in unison.

It was like coming home. This is what sex was supposed to be like, and he hadn't realized how much he'd missed the intimacy until just then.

"I love you so goddamn much," he growled as he began making rhythmic thrusts.

Again, she *hmphed* in response.

Jacob paused and looked down at her.

"What? I do. And you know it. And I also think, deep down, you still love me, too."

"I don't want to have this conversation right now, Jake," she said, tugging on his ass to encourage him to continue. "Fuck me. Please."

Given how he'd ended things last time, he understood her reluctance to believe him. He needed to serve his penance—he knew that. He just couldn't help saying how he felt when he was balls deep inside her.

So, instead of continuing to profess his love with words, he began to express it with his body, making love to her.

It was not at all what she wanted.

"Harder!"

Jacob increased the pace, but it was still not to her satisfaction, because she grabbed a fistful of his hair, and through gritted teeth, snarled, "Harder, dammit!"

It was the sexiest thing she'd ever done, and his cock was like a steel rod.

He began to thrust faster, his balls slapping against her ass as he slammed into her. Taren lifted her legs and began to fondle her clit as he proceeded to pound her cunt like he hated her. He realized as he pumped into her furiously, this really was a hate fuck on her part.

As unhappy as he was to be the object of her loathing, the act itself was erotic as hell, and he was already close to coming. When she came undone underneath him, grabbing her tits and arching her back like a fucking porn star, he roared his release—holding her hips and slamming into her as deep as he could while he emptied his cock.

Breathing heavily, he fell forward, catching himself on his forearms and tried to kiss her again.

This time, she turned her head.

****

Taren

What am I doing?

Not only was she having sex with *Jacob Smith*, she had been completely unabashed. Everything about this situation was like something from her dreams—the fantasies she'd had in her head when David was on top of her.

Except her fantasies hadn't come close to how good reality was.

She'd spent the last seven years wondering why Jacob had left her. He'd given her some bullshit about his job, but she hadn't believed it. He wouldn't admit there was someone else, but in her heart, she knew there was. Why else would he just end it when things were going so great between them? Not only end it, but disappear from her life without another word—ever again, until this afternoon. He'd changed his number, had no digital presence—anywhere. She'd looked on more than one occasion, and since she'd never once been to his house, she had no idea how to physically find him. She thought maybe he'd found someone with more sexual prowess who was sure of herself. Taren had been completely inexperienced before Jake. Although she had always been up for whatever he wanted to try, in or out of the bedroom, she knew she had been timid when it came to initiating anything.

When he broke up with her out of the blue.... Devastated didn't come close to describing how she felt that fateful day, and for months and even years later—although she eventually managed to function again and get on with life.

Time had allowed her some perspective, and she was eventually able to look back on their time together and smile. He'd told her from the beginning he wasn't forever material, she'd just naively thought she could make him love her enough to change his mind. They were together for three blissful years—albeit sporadically because his consulting job required him to travel a lot. Still, it was long enough that she'd gotten comfortable and believed they were headed toward marriage and babies.

Instead, she married David Graham four years later.

Now, here she was, divorced and naked with Jacob.

Again, how the hell did I get here?

Regardless of how amazing the sex had just been, she wasn't getting sucked back into Jake's web. Her heart couldn't handle it.

His arms were wrapped around her, and he was nuzzling her hair, murmuring sweet nothings. He was strong and beautiful, and she remembered the times before when lying with him after he'd rocked her world had brought her such contentment. Taren was *this* close to closing her eyes and allowing herself those old feelings. It would be so easy to do.

With resolve she never knew she had, she sat up, breaking the spell he was lulling her into. Escaping to the bathroom, she cleaned up, put her robe on that she'd hung up on the bathroom hook when she unpacked, brushed her hair and wiped away any stray mascara before returning to find him with one arm behind his head, still naked in her bed.

Jacob threw the sheet back and patted the space next to him. Instead of meeting his demands this time, she shook her head with a sad smile and said, "I think you should go now."

He tilted his head to the side and eyed her, as if trying to decide whether or not she was serious.

"Why don't you come back to bed and let me hold you a while longer."

She winced and closed her eyes. *That sounds heavenly.*

"I can't."

He got out of bed, his flaccid cock, still huge compared to her ex's, bobbed as he approached her. He was male perfection personified.

She'd never admit it—not even to herself, but she felt a sense of relief when he wrapped his arms around her instead of reaching for his clothes.

"Tinkerbell, let me stay with you. Please? I need to hold you, baby."

She sank into his embrace. Reveled in it. It was like the world made sense again being in his arms.

Except.

Except he'd left her without warning seven years ago and turned her world upside down. Then nothing had seemed to make sense. She wasn't going through that again.

"I can't, Jake. I'm just getting my bearings again. You can't come waltzing back into my life and think everything's going to be the same. You had your chance with me, and you chose to throw it away." Tears filled her eyes as she pulled away from him. "Please go."

The hurt look on his face almost made her relent, but she didn't. She stood her ground. No good could come from him staying the night.

He dressed quickly and pulled her back into his arms, as if giving her one last chance to change her mind. She didn't, and he dropped a kiss on her forehead.

"I'm back for good, Taren. Let me prove it to you. Breakfast tomorrow? Eight o'clock? I'll pick you up."

Her head was swimming. She should say no. But there was no way she didn't want to see more of him, even though she knew better.

She heard herself whisper, "Okay."

He planted a long kiss in her hair as he hugged her tight, not seeming to be in a hurry to let go. When he finally did, he softly said, "I love you, Tink," then walked out the door.

Leaving her almost as confused as he had seven years ago.

Chapter Four

Jacob

The last thing he wanted to do was leave her cabin. But she'd asked him to go, so he thought it would be in his best interest to honor her request. Although it was tempting as hell to disregard it and just make her listen to him.

Not the right approach. If there was one thing he excelled at, it was knowing the right way to deal with any situation. That skill had made him incredibly wealthy.

He went next door to his room and fired up his secure laptop and WiFi to do some work. He was working on a few things that were coming to a head later this week, and he still needed to direct things from behind the scenes. It was times like this that being a lone wolf really sucked; he didn't have anyone else to pick up the slack so he could go on a real vacation, or god forbid, if he got sick—which was rare. However, until now, he hadn't even remotely been on a vacation in seven years—it'd always just been working from a more exotic locale than New Orleans. He didn't even have an assistant, although he was seriously considering getting one now that Taren was going to be occupying his time.

Jacob had opened the door leading to the balcony so he could hear if she went out on hers. He heard voices and peeked his head out to see dinner being delivered to her table outside. Come to think of it, he was hungry, too, so he picked up the phone on the desk and also requested room service—

offering a hundred-dollar tip if his sandwich was there in less than ten minutes. That did the trick because the steward delivered his food to the table on his balcony in nine. He handed the man a hundred-dollar bill while thanking him on his way out, grabbed a beer from the mini fridge, and walked outside to find her sitting in a chair, staring at the ocean with a wine glass in her hand. None of the food on her plate seemed to have been touched.

She gasped and almost dropped her glass when he asked, "Penny for your thoughts."

Penny for your thoughts? Did I really just say that?

With narrowed eyes, she accused, "You're next door? Isn't that convenient."

If she thought he'd be sheepish or ashamed, she should have known better.

"I thought so. I especially like the adjoining door between our cabins so we don't even have to go out in the hall to be together."

Taren shook her head, a small smile forming on her lips. "Have you no shame? Do you even know how to be contrite?"

He was leaning on the railing now, as close to her balcony as he could physically get.

"When it comes to you? No, I have no shame. And yes, I do know how to be contrite—I'll do my penance as long it takes to win you back. But we both know I'm not going to get you to marry me without taking some bold measures."

She choked on her wine, her hand going to her chest as she sputtered, "Marry you? You've got to be kidding me!"

"Not even a little bit, Tinkerbell."

She stared at him for a minute, then began to swirl the Riesling around in her glass as she looked out at the moonlit waves.

"You've got some pretty big *cajones*. I'll give you that, Jake."

The better to fuck you with, baby.

He lifted his chin toward her plate.

"Why aren't you eating?"

"I don't have much of an appetite."

"Because of me?"

She shrugged. "I guess."

"Why?"

Shooting him a look of disbelief, she asked, "Did you seriously just ask me, *why*?"

Unapologetic, he nodded. "Yeah, why?"

He must have hit a nerve because she set her glass down harshly and shot out of her chair, with one hand on her hip while she thrust her finger in his direction.

"Do you have any idea what it did to me when you left? *Any* idea?"

Jacob had already known she didn't leave her house for a month after he broke up with her, but he knew he wasn't going to like hearing it from her, and was feeling queasy about where this conversation was going. He hung his head and whispered, "I'm sorry."

"You're sorry?" Her voice went up an octave. "You're *sorry*? I couldn't get out of bed for a month. I lost fifteen pounds. I couldn't sleep. I couldn't eat. I didn't care whether I lived or died. In fact, there were times I wanted to die because I just wanted to stop hurting. It took me years—*years*, Jacob—to even trust a man enough to go on a date again."

He didn't know how to respond. "I'm so sorry."

She glossed over his apology. "So now you want me to just forget all that and pretend it never happened and pick up right where we left off?"

"No," he said in a low voice. "I know I have a lot to make up for. I know I have to earn your forgiveness. I told you, I'm prepared to do whatever I have to do, for as long as it takes until I have your trust again."

She folded her arms, pushing her boobs up. It took every bit of his willpower not to stare.

"Why now, Jake?"

He tilted his head. "What do you mean?"

She appeared to be enjoying their power shift and her demeanor reflected it. *Enjoy it while it lasts, my little fairy.*

She tossed her hair and repeated herself like he was hard of hearing. "*Why. Now.* Why, after seven years are you back? What's changed? Did you get tired of my replacement?"

That got his ire up, and he found himself raising his voice. "First of all, there was no fucking replacement. I haven't been in a relationship since you, Taren."

That seemed to catch her off guard and tempered her attitude, momentarily at least. She quickly glanced away and picked up her wine glass and began to fidget with the stem.

"So why then?" she whispered softly.

Jacob sighed. He knew he was going to have to tell her the whole dirty truth about his life, but not yet. It would be way too much, too soon, for her to take in. Instead, he vaguely replied, "Because I couldn't go one more day without you. I wasn't going to miss my opportunity when I learned you were single again."

"Yeah, about that. I find it hard to believe that your timing was so perfect that you started looking for me right when I became divorced."

"Tinkerbell, I've always kept an eye on you, in one form or another."

"What the hell is that supposed to mean?"

He should have known she wouldn't let him say something cryptic like that without demanding more information. *Idiot.*

"It means I've always made sure you were safe and doing okay."

"Oh my god, you're talking in circles. If you're not going to be straight with me, our conversation is done."

She set her glass down then turned to leave and he called after her, "Wait!" causing her to stop and slowly turn back around, arms crossed at her chest again. This time, he took his time staring at her tits before lifting his eyes to meet hers. He could only grovel so much.

"What do you want to know?"

She flung her arms down in exasperation, causing her boobs to bounce. "I swear to god, Jake... You already fucking know what I want to know."

He knew she was really pissed when she started to swear. Time to provide some information as a peace offering. She wasn't going to like it.

"I have a private investigator on my payroll check on you occasionally and provide me with reports and photos."

"A private investigator? Following me? For how long?"

He shrugged nonchalantly. "About a week after I left, I had someone check on you every couple of months; I just wanted to make sure you were doing okay. When you started dating *him*, I stopped—I couldn't stand seeing you two together. Except I couldn't stay away and started checking on you every so often. Last year, you looked so sad, and a friend of mine said something that stuck with me... I've been keeping regular track of you ever since."

"What did your friend say?"

"That just because you'd moved on, didn't mean he was the better man for you. I knew my friend was right. No one would be better for you than me."

Tears were flowing down her face.

"You son-of-a-bitch. Of course he wasn't the better man for me, but *you* didn't want me, remember?"

"Tink... it wasn't that I—"

She held her hand in the universal 'stop' gesture and shook her head.

"No, save it. You left. You disappeared and never contacted me again. Don't you *dare* tell me you wanted me. If you wanted me, you would have had me. Just because you kept track of me doesn't mean shit." She turned on her heel toward her cabin but stopped and looked back at him. "I don't want to see you again. Stay away from me."

And with that, she walked inside and closed the door. He heard the *click* of the lock catching and threw his head back with a sigh. *So much for being honest with her. Fuck!*

****

Taren

He's been 'keeping an eye on me' for seven years? Seven fucking years? And he never once reached out to me? Not once? Fuck him.

Chapter Five

Taren

She made sure she was up and gone before 8:00 a.m. Her anger had dissipated with sleep, and she knew she wouldn't be strong enough to resist him if he showed up at her door to take her to breakfast.

So she spent the day at the spa where she'd be guaranteed not to run into him, since it wasn't co-ed. Massage, haircut, manicure, pedicure, steam room, whirlpool, facial… she'd done it all. If you're going to hide out for the day, Taren would definitely recommend that as the place to do so.

She didn't know what to make of Jake keeping track of her all these years. Last night, she was livid that he'd been keeping tabs on her but never bothered to actually see her. What was the point then? And how unfair was it that he got to know what she was doing, but she'd no idea what or who he was doing—or where. Or even if he were still alive.

Still, learning that, a small part of her felt… loved? How messed up was that? But it was that feeling that kept the anger at bay and let her enjoy her day.

Feeling relaxed as she made her way through the ship's hallways in the big, fluffy, white robe and disposable sandals given to her at the spa, she started planning her evening. Dinner, then the comedy club show, and maybe after that, if she wasn't too tired, she'd check out the nightclub. She was mentally going through her wardrobe choices when she opened her cabin door and stopped short. There he was sitting on her couch in grey dress slacks and a white button down with the sleeves rolled to the elbows to showcase his ridiculously expensive watch, Scotch in hand. His other arm was thrown along the back of the cushions, left foot on his right knee, perched like he owned the place. She should have been expecting this.

"Look, Jake," she snarled as the door closed behind her. "Just because you paid for my trip doesn't mean you can come into my room uninvited."

"I was worried maybe you'd jumped ship. Glad to see that's not the case. I'll be sure to have your spa day charged to my room, since I have a feeling I was the cause of you needing it."

"Don't flatter yourself," she scoffed as she opened the wardrobe door.

She felt his presence behind her, and he reached in front of her to pull out her mint green dress.

"Wear this one," he instructed in her ear. "With your new haircut, you'll definitely look like my Tinkerbell."

She took the dress from him and hung it back up, pulling out the black one instead and walking toward the bathroom. Dammit, she'd actually been planning on wearing the green one.

"I'm not your Tinkerbell. Not anymore," she said flatly before pulling the door shut behind her.

"Yes, you are. You'll always be mine."

****

Jacob

"You should've thought about that before you dumped me seven years ago," she sassily called from the other side of the locked door.

"Someday I'll explain it all to you, and you'll understand I had no choice," he answered vaguely.

She opened the door a crack and peered out at him.

"Someday? Why not now?"

"Because…" and she promptly closed the door in his face, relocking it once she did.

"Blah, blah, blah. Until you're ready to explain this bullshit to me, we have nothing left to talk about. You can go now; you've seen I haven't jumped ship and am *safe and sound.*" She cracked the door again and eyed him with disdain, "That is your specialty, isn't it? Making sure I'm safe and sound but leaving me alone."

He moved toward the door, and she quickly slammed it and locked it again.

"You're awfully brave behind a locked door, little one."

Wisely, she didn't take the bait and remained in her perceived safety. Not that the flimsy latch could have kept him out if he'd really wanted to get to her. But he needed to play nice if he desired any chance of being with her. Last night on the balcony had been a severe setback, and he only had eight more days before they returned to San Diego where they'd both get on a plane. If he wanted it to be to the same destination, he needed to behave. His sexual prowess was only going to get him so far with her; although yesterday's escapade had been pretty goddamn amazing. She'd certainly seemed to enjoy it—right up until she'd kicked him to the curb, that is.

"Hurry up, would ya? I'm starving."

Taren opened the door, completely dressed and utterly stunning.

"I'm not having dinner with you," she stated matter-of-factly as she walked into the room, opened a drawer, and pulled out a traveling jewelry box. He peered over her shoulder at her jewelry and saw a tennis bracelet he had once given her. Reaching around her, he plucked it out of the grey velvet case, wrapped it tenderly around her wrist, and fastened the clasp.

"I'm glad to see you've kept this and still wear it," he said in a low voice, completely ignoring her declaration that she wasn't having dinner with him, and slowly stroking his thumb in circles along her inner wrist, one of her erogenous zones if he remembered correctly.

She snatched her hand back and rubbed her wrist vigorously where he'd been caressing. "Pffft, I don't still wear this."

"Then why'd you bring it with you?"

"I—I must have grabbed it out of my jewelry armoire by accident."

He smirked and put his hand in his pocket as he casually leaned against the wall. "Sure, Tink. Whatever you say."

"Then... then, I guess I forgot you were the one to give it to me."

He knew she was trying to wound him. If he thought for a second she was telling the truth, she might have.

With a smug grin, he replied, "No, you didn't."

She stammered for a comeback and seemed at a loss for something clever to say, so Jacob seized on the opportunity.

"Shall we go to dinner?"

She appeared so rattled about the bracelet, she didn't even argue with him as he escorted her out the door with his hand on the small of her back.

Chapter Six

Taren

Damn that man. He thinks he's so clever.

She loved her diamond bracelet; even after being dumped by him, she never traveled without it. She hardly ever wore it, but to her, it was her lucky charm—which was ironic considering how unlucky she'd been without him. It didn't take a psychology degree to figure out why she felt the attachment to the inanimate object. It symbolized a time when Jacob was by her side, and she'd felt like she could conquer the world.

Taren never discussed Jacob after they broke up. Ever. So if someone only met her in the last seven years, they wouldn't know anything about him. David didn't have a clue he'd even existed, so her husband never questioned when she would occasionally wear a piece of jewelry he'd given her. But Jake was never far from her thoughts.

Reflecting on it, she realized her marriage hadn't stood a chance. The ghost of Jacob Smith had always been there in the background. She'd find herself comparing David to Jake, and unfortunately, her husband never measured up. Before she even married him, she'd come to terms that he'd never compare to her first love—but he was there for her, and Jacob wasn't. Then she discovered his affairs—plural, and with her friends, no less. That's when she knew it was time to end things. Unfortunately, it took a while to find the courage and strength to go through with it. The new job definitely helped; she wouldn't have to rely on anyone to pay her rent if she left, not to mention the confidence boost it'd given her to have a headhunter call her out of the blue, saying someone had passed her resume on to him and would she be interested in talking.

She'd worn the tennis bracelet to the headhunter interview and walked out with a job offer with a salary and benefits she'd never even imagined. When the paperwork was official and her signing bonus hit her new checking account after she'd made it past her ninety days' probation, she filed for divorce.

She stopped short and turned to Jake.

The pieces were falling into place.

"You're the one who sent my resume to the headhunter, aren't you?"

He looked at her with a blank face, obviously trying to decipher the best way to answer.

Finally, he touched her elbow gently and said, "Don't be mad. I didn't do much, just made a few calls."

It was tempting to milk the situation, but she didn't have the heart. Besides, she had plenty of other things for leverage right now.

Instead, she lovingly cupped his cheek. Obviously not what he was expecting, because he flinched. She'd never slap him, although he probably knew he deserved it. But not for this.

With a small smile, she looked into his beautiful green eyes and said, "Thank you," before standing on her tiptoes and kissing the other side of his face softly.

When she was flatfooted again—well, as flatfooted as she could be in heels, his hand slid around her waist, and he bent down to murmur in her ear, "I'm the better man for you, Tink. Let me prove it."

She closed her eyes and pressed against him.

"I don't think my heart would survive being broken again by you, Jake."

"Mine neither, baby," he said, resting his cheek on top of her head while running his fingers up and down her back. "Mine neither."

****

Jacob

She didn't pull away from his embrace—that was a start. And she'd kept his bracelet. The one he'd given her the first time he'd told her he loved her.

"What do you say we play a little game?" she said as they started walking toward the restaurant.

With one eyebrow raised, he suspiciously asked, "What kind of game?"

"Let's pretend we're meeting for the first time tonight. No baggage from our past."

He liked that idea—*a lot.*

"Okay."

"But."

Of course there was a *but*.

"We can't lie about anything."

"Can we choose not to answer?"

"Sure. But, keep in mind, this is your first time meeting me. Do you want to see me again? If so, answer accordingly. I'm not going to go out on a second date with someone sketchy who won't answer simple questions about himself."

"Well, if this is your first time meeting me, I would hope you're not going to get *too* personal with your questions."

"We'll see where the night takes us," she said with a coy smile as they approached the hostess stand.

They stood to the side and waited to be seated, and he leaned over to whisper in her ear, "I'm not sure if I've told you this already, but you look stunning tonight. Good enough to eat."

She shot him an admonishing look.

"Would you really say that to someone you just met?"

He hesitated, and she held her hand up as she shook her head in disgust. "Don't answer that."

"You're right, I wouldn't. I'm sorry. But you do look beautiful. And I love your haircut; it reminds me of Tinkerbell."

That made her smile.

"I've been told that."

He loved that she'd cut her hair in the pixie-style he was used to on her. She was beautiful with longer hair, of course, but the new cut was more his old Tink.

"Any reason you decided to get it cut?"

"My ex-husband hated my hair short. When I sat down in the stylist's chair today, and she asked me what I wanted, I realized what *I* wanted was to wear it short again."

"You should always do what you want."

"I think I'm just now realizing what a pleaser I really am."

"Sometimes being a pleaser isn't a bad thing," he said with a flirtatious smile and wink.

"No," she flirted back. "Sometimes pleasing can be oh-so satisfying."

And, just like that, his dick was hard.

Tonight was going to be interesting, that was for sure.

Chapter Seven

Jacob

They were seated and waiting on their drink order, perusing the menu, when she asked, "What looks good?"

He broke out into a wicked grin as he looked her over from her sexy tits to her adorable face and back down to her tits again.

"*On the menu.*"

"Oh, sorry. I think I'm going to have the New York Strip. You?"

"Hmm, tough choice, but I'm going to go with the fettuccine alfredo."

"Can I interest you in sharing?"

They used to do that all the time when they went out to eat.

She broke out into a big smile. "I'd love that."

He needed to keep reminding her of their good times.

"So, Jacob Smith. What do you do?"

No lies. Shit. Were they really going to do this?

Maybe it was a good thing. He'd promised himself he was going to tell her *everything*.

Calmly, like he was explaining he worked at Target, he said, "I used to work for the government, but I retired about four years ago and am a troubleshooting consultant now."

He saw her wheels turning.

"The government? I thought you were—" she asked with a tilted head, her brows furrowed in confusion.

With one eyebrow raised, he cut her off, reiterating slowly, "The government, Tink."

The light bulb went on, and he nodded his head as her expression changed when what he meant hit her, just as the waiter approached with their wine.

She waited until the server walked away, then dramatically looked around to see if anyone had been listening to their conversation. He'd have to work with her on her covert skills.

"And now you're a *troubleshooting consultant*? Who are your clients?" she whispered harshly.

Jacob casually lifted his wine glass, pausing mid-air as he contemplated her question, then answered before taking a drink, "Different government agencies, some countries, some private individuals."

Her eyes were wide as she stared at him.

"Is it dangerous work?" Her voice was low now, and she kept looking around.

"It can be. Fortunately, my fee is pretty high and that affords me tight security, among other things."

"Other things?"

He shrugged. "A private jet, remote locations when I travel, access to some pretty important people..."

"Have you ever killed anyone?"

"I'm afraid I'm going to have to play my *I'd rather not answer* card."

"Is that why you left me?"

He smirked over the rim of his glass.

"Why, Taren, I just met you tonight; I don't know what you mean by that."

She narrowed her eyes and folded her arms.

"Have you ever been married?"

Sneaky girl.

"No." He knew where she was going with this.

"Have you ever been close?"

"There was a girl I loved with all my heart about seven years ago. Then a colleague's wife was murdered in revenge for something we'd done. Even though I'd done a decent job of keeping our relationship hidden, there wasn't a chance in hell I was going to risk her getting killed."

Tears welled up in her eyes.

"You should have told me," she whispered.

The game was over.

He reached for her hand and squeezed. "I couldn't, baby."

"If you'd had, at least your leaving me would have made sense. I wouldn't have sat up night after night wondering what I'd done wrong."

Jacob didn't have a lot of regrets in life, but how he ended things with her was right up there at number one. He'd left her devastated, and it had all but gutted him. When she didn't heal and move on like he'd hoped, it weighed even heavier on him. Then she married that asshole.

He wanted to scoop her up into his lap and rock her against him. He settled for caressing his thumb over her hand as he held it, only letting go when their dinner was served.

She scraped half her pasta onto his plate while he was busy cutting his steak in half.

"I wish I would have done so many things differently, Tinkerbell. But to be fair, my heart was breaking too, and I wasn't exactly thinking straight."

She paused mid-bite and asked, "So, what's changed? What makes you think my life wouldn't be in danger now?"

"I don't think that," he stated matter-of-factly, sliding her half of his dinner onto her plate. "But I have the resources now to ensure your safety."

"And you didn't back then?"

"Not like I do now."

Her face was twisted as she processed everything he'd just disclosed.

"What if I don't think I can live like that?"

"Then I'll respect your wishes and go back to making sure you're safe from afar."

"You wouldn't try to talk me into being with you?"

The way she said it, like the idea he'd give up so easily hurt her feelings, made him pause.

"That depends."

"On?"

"On whether or not I think there's a shot you'd eventually say yes."

She bit her bottom lip nervously.

"And what would make you think that you had a shot?"

Staring into her eyes, he replied with a smirk, "I can think of a few things."

She quickly looked away, a smile forming on her lips as a blush crept across her cheeks.

"Oh."

"So, Taren Fairchild, what do you do?"

****

Taren

Holy shit.

Holy fucking shit.

Jacob was a spy?

Jacob was a spy!

Suddenly, things made sense. His secretiveness, how he'd never answer her questions about his job, why she never once went to his house in the three years they were together, why she'd never met any of his friends or family—other than his brother, and why he wasn't exactly thrilled at the prospect of meeting hers. And so many other little things.

He. Was. A. Secret Agent.

Was, past tense?

It kind of sounded like he still was, in some capacity.

Was it wrong that she was turned on?

Yes! She hadn't really known him *at all*. She couldn't be having horny feelings for him at a time like this.

But damn... a secret agent? That was sexy as hell.

He tried restarting their game of pretend but there were some things she needed to know first.

"We'll get back to playing in a minute. I have some more questions."

"Understandable," he nodded and gestured with his utensils in his hands. "Proceed."

"Was anything real? Between us, I mean?"

His expression was pained as he set the knife and fork down and reached for her again.

"Baby, you were the *only* thing real in my life."

"But everything you told me was a lie."

"No," he quickly corrected her. "I lied about what I did for a living. Everything else was the honest-to-god truth."

"I feel like I don't even know you."

"Taren," he said in an exasperated tone as he briefly looked at the ceiling. "Outside of my family, *you* are the only person who does know me."

She let that sink in until she finally whispered, "So what now?"

He picked up his utensils like he was going to continue his dinner.

"How about we spend the next eight days getting to know each other again, and go from there?"

"Do you promise to be one hundred percent honest with me for the rest of the cruise?"

"I promise to be honest with you for the rest of my life."

"One hundred percent?"

"How about ninety-eight? You've got to leave me a little wiggle room in case I don't like your cooking or I'm planning a surprise party or something."

She tried not to smile. This wasn't the time for jokes, dammit, he needed to be serious.

"Okay, but not about the big stuff."

He nodded solemnly. "Not about the big stuff."

"Okay then." She refolded the crease in the napkin in her lap then reached for her wine glass. "To answer your earlier question, I'm an ER nurse at Houston Methodist Hospital, but I was just offered a new position in—"

Setting her drink down with a *thud, she* sat back in her chair and glared at him.

"Where are you living right now?"

"New Orleans."

She folded her arms across her chest.

"You wouldn't happen to have had anything to do with the job offer I just got from East Jefferson General Hospital, would you?"

He looked like he'd been caught with his hand in the cookie jar as he glanced down.

"I might have made a few calls," he said before taking a bite of food.

"First the headhunter, and then this? You can't just go around manipulating my life," she hissed.

He set his fork down with a *clang*.

"Hold on, one second. I didn't manipulate your life. I made sure opportunities were presented to you—that's all. You've had complete free will whether to accept or reject them. I had no influence in *your* decision. Any job you choose to take, or not take, is completely up to you."

"How convenient that the latest opportunity you made sure to be presented is in the city where you live."

"It is very convenient." He picked his fork back up. "I'm not going to apologize for wanting you closer to me, Tink. But it's up to you whether you accept the position or not."

"You have an answer for everything, don't you?"

"It's why I get paid the big bucks," he replied with a grin then took another bite of his dinner.

Damn him and his sexy face.

Chapter Eight

Jacob

Talk about laying his cards on the table.

She'd responded better than he'd thought, which led to him having more regret about how he'd handled things in the past. He should have been honest with her seven years ago; the agency's rules be damned.

He should have done a lot of things differently, but he was willing to cut himself some slack. His forty-year-old self was a lot smarter than his thirty-three-year-old self. Same could probably be said for Tink. Who knows how the twenty-three-year-old Taren would have handled what he'd just told her.

"So what should we do next?" he asked as the waiter cleared their dessert dishes. "Want to go to the lido deck and see what's going on there?"

"That sounds fun."

His hand was at the small of her back as they left the restaurant, but when they stepped outside, he reached for her hand without thinking—as if out of habit. And just like she used to, she entwined her fingers with his.

It was funny, but that simple act caused a sense of peace to come over him. Because he knew in that moment, she still loved him, and they'd figure out a way to make this relationship work.

Eventually.

Right now, he still had a penance to serve.

They reached the lido deck to find a DJ playing a pop song, and people having a great time drinking, dancing, and doing—of all things, the limbo.

He was standing behind her and leaned down close to her ear. "You should do that; I bet you'd win."

Looking over her shoulder at him with a smirk, she asked, "Why do you bet I'd win?"

Grinning, he said, "I don't know. You look flexible."

She rolled her eyes, so he couldn't help himself. His hand came around to the front of her hips, and he pulled her back into him so she could feel his hard cock against her ass.

"I already know how flexible you really are, baby," he whispered in her ear, then subtly pressed his dick harder against her. He fought back a smile when he felt her push back.

"If I reached under this dress, would I find your panties wet?"

She shook her head, and he said in a low voice. "Lying isn't permitted tonight, remember?"

"I'm not—I'm not lying," she stammered.

"Taren Scarlett Fairchild," he growled. "Yes, you are."

"No, I'm not."

"Okay, then. How about I take you to a deserted spot on deck right now and feel your panties? If they're wet, you have to spend the night with me. Every night. For the rest of the cruise."

"And what happens when you don't find them wet?"

"Baby girl, we both know that's not going to happen. But, if by some miracle, your panties are dry, I'll do whatever you want."

"Anything I want?"

"You name it."

He was already tugging her to the empty part of the deck that was dark and secluded.

"Anything I want?" she reiterated.

Something wasn't right. She was too confident.

"What do you want?"

"I want a back and foot massage." She pointed her finger at him. "And *only* a back and foot massage, every night."

"Tinkerbell, you don't have to win a bet for me to give you a massage. All you have to do is ask. I'd be happy to." He tilted his head. "Didn't you get one at the spa today?"

"Yes, but no one gives better massages than you. And it's been so long. All I was thinking about the entire time she was massaging me was how much better you are at it."

That made his ego swell a little. But it quickly deflated because he now knew he was going to lose the bet without even checking. He'd been so sure that she was as turned on as he was. Was he losing his touch?

He backed her into a dark corner and reached under her dress. His middle finger probed between her legs and found her drenched.

"You *were* lying," he snarled as he began to slide his digit inside her soaked pussy and slowly finger fuck her.

She was having trouble talking, but she managed to stammer out, "No, I wasn't. You said wet *panties*."

That's when it dawned on him that she wasn't wearing any, and his cock almost punched a hole through his zipper.

"You sneaky little minx," he growled and curved his finger inside her, yanking her dress waist high so she was completely exposed. "I'm going to have to punish you for that."

"Punish me? H—h—how?"

He began to jackrabbit his hand between her legs, his curled finger ramming deep inside her.

"You're going to squirt for me, naughty girl."

His arm wrapped her middle so he could hold on to her when her knees gave out. It also allowed him to play with her clit with his other hand.

"Wh-at?" she panted. "No! I can't—I've never... Ohhh fuck!"

He yanked his finger from her pussy as she began squirting all over the deck, but continued vigorously rubbing her clit. He began finger fucking her again, hard, intending to make her squirt and come at the same time.

Minutes later, she did just that, chanting, "Oh my god, oh my god, oh my god... Yessss!" and just like he predicted, her knees buckled. He bent his legs to help catch her, then scooped her up in his arms and sat down on a nearby deck chair with her still in his embrace.

"I've got you, baby," he whispered as he smoothed her hair from her face and kissed her forehead. "I've got you..."

She was like a ragdoll in his lap, limp and pliant against his chest. They sat there like that for a long time, Jacob gently rocking her as he kissed her reverently.

Finally, she softly murmured, "I can't believe you just did that."

Suddenly he froze. She'd always been adventurous yet deliciously submissive, but there were some boundaries they hadn't crossed before.

"Did I go too far?"

He felt her shake her head.

"No. I loved it. If it were anyone else, I'd be embarrassed by how much. I just didn't think I could, you know, do that."

"You mean squirt?" he said smugly.

"Yes, that." It was kind of adorable how she wouldn't say it.

"Well, I'm glad you liked it because it was sexy as fuck to watch, and I'm definitely going to want to do it again soon."

"Mmm," she purred and nestled closer to him.

"Come on, beautiful. Let's go back to your room."

He helped her off his lap then stood up and wrapped his arm around her, delighted when she wrapped both hers around his middle and laid her head on his shoulder.

"I know I cheated," she giggled, as if proud of herself. "So I think you should still spend the night."

"Was already planning on it, baby."

Chapter Nine

Taren

They were back in her room, Taren still a little shaky from what just happened on deck, when Jacob advised, "I'll be right back," then slipped through the door adjoining their cabins. He returned moments later with a jar of coconut oil, two glasses, and a bottle of champagne.

"Wow, those are, um, quite the party favors you've got there."

He ignored her and concentrated on opening the champagne. The cork on the bottle popped, and he poured two glasses, handing her one.

She took a sip, the bubbles tickling her tongue. It was good—probably expensive.

"Take off your clothes."

She almost spewed champagne everywhere, but managed to choke it down before snarking, "Excuse me? You're not even going to romance me first? Just, *let's get to it*? This isn't making me want to run away with you, ya know."

He shot her a look.

"I was going to give you a massage, smart mouth. But I might just bend you over my knee and paint your ass red instead if you keep it up with the sass."

That made her pussy clench. He'd never spanked her before, but the idea was erotic.

He leaned in with a chuckle. "Your nipples are hard, Tink. Does that mean you like that idea?"

"I don't know," she whispered with her lips against the glass as she tried to visualize it. "I've never been spanked before. Not even when I was a little girl."

"Well, keep being a brat, little one, and there will be a first time for everything."

This was a new side to Jacob. He'd always been in charge, but this was next level. She kind of liked it, until she realized he'd probably acquired this new taste with someone else.

"I'm afraid you'll just have to play your spanking fantasies out with your other girlfriends when we get back."

The angry look he gave her made her heart lodge in her throat, and she swallowed hard when he barked, "Clothes. Off. Now!"

She scrambled to do what he ordered while he made a show of removing his belt from his pants. Her dress was off, and he was sitting on the bed watching her try to remove her bra with trembling fingers.

"Come here," he ordered in a softer tone.

Taren stood before him, and he turned her around to unclasp her bra, gently pulling it from her body, then turned her back around. She was completely naked. Exposed. Vulnerable. And a little bit scared.

Jacob grabbed her wrist and tugged her into his lap.

"Other than you, I have not had a girlfriend in the last twenty years. You're the only woman I fantasize about. I'm not going to tell you I've been living like a monk, because I promised I wouldn't lie to you, but it never meant anything to me. Sex with you *means* something—even when it's dirty and taboo. Maybe *especially when* it's dirty and taboo. Don't think for a second that I'm ever going to be with another woman now that you're back in my life, and definitely don't suggest it." He paused and raised an eyebrow. "Unless you were trying to get spanked?"

"No, I wasn't trying to get spanked," she retorted defiantly. "How was I supposed to know you don't have other girlfriends?"

A low growl escaped his throat. "You really do want to be bent over my knee, don't you? You honestly think I would try to get you back while having another girlfriend?"

"I don't know, Jake. Maybe? It's not like I really know you."

She was deliberately pushing him now. Part of her wanted to see if he'd really go through with putting her over his knee, and part of her wanted to see how far she could push.

Apparently, not very far.

"Wrong answer," he snarled and lifted her off his lap, then patted it. "Ass up."

"You can't be serious."

He didn't reply, just glared at her in warning.

"I changed my mind," she pouted as she bent over his lap. "I don't think you should spend the night."

"Too bad," he responded, dismissing her. "I suggest you stop talking or your punishment is just going to get worse."

He rubbed her ass, and she felt a sudden sense of panic and decided to try one last approach. Running her hand over his thigh, she wiggled her ass suggestively as she slid off his lap onto her knees, murmuring, "I'm sorry." She began to mouth his cock over his pants and looked up at him demurely. "Can't we just skip the spanking? Surely there's another way I can show you how sorry I am."

He didn't respond, just sat watching her, so she began to undo his pants. He subtly lifted his hips as she began tugging them and his boxer briefs down his thighs until his cock sprang free.

"I know I was a naughty girl," she said as she looked up at him while stroking his cock. "So bad"—then swirled her tongue around his tip before rubbing his shaft against her cheek—"I know I still need to be punished. Can't you think of some other way?"

"You dirty little slut," he snarled, grabbing a handful of her hair and pulling her head back so she was forced to look at him. "You want me to fuck that sweet little mouth of yours as punishment instead, baby?"

"Mmm hmm," she whimpered. "Please, Jake. Fuck my face."

He released her hair as he closed his eyes and threw his head back, muttering, "Fuuuuck!"

Exactly the effect she wanted to have on him.

He traced her lips with the tip of his cock, smearing the precum around like lipstick.

"This is the only time your ploy will work, little one. Next time, you're getting spanked."

She furrowed her brow. "What if I don't want to be spanked? Ever."

He smirked. "Okay, then we'll have to think of some other way to punish your ass. I have a few ideas." His expression turned serious. "Do you really not want to be spanked?"

She swirled her tongue around his helmet and looked up at him with a coy smile. "I didn't say *that*. I just wanted to know I have a say."

"You'll always have a say."

"Well, I say you should punish my mouth with your cock."

****

Jacob

When did his sweet Tinkerbell turn into such a vixen? He fucking loved it.

Although he wasn't wild about the idea of her doing this with anyone else. However, simply based on six of his last seven years, it was probably better if he didn't ask. This last year he'd been celibate; ever since the day he thought there was a chance that maybe, someday soon, she'd be back in his life.

As she deep throated his cock, he closed his eyes with a smug smile. That *someday* was *now*. And it was fucking glorious.

Now, he had a punishment to mete out that she was begging for, and he was more than happy to oblige. The fact that he was the one who was actually supposed to be serving a penance was not lost on him.

He grabbed her hair and began to maneuver her mouth, pushing her deep until her nose touched his groin, and he held her there.

"Mmm, that's right. Swallow that cock."

He pulled her off, and she gasped for air. A string of spit ran from her mouth to his cock and her mascara was smeared from her watery eyes.

"You were a bad girl," he said through gritted teeth as he held her head in place by her hair and began to fuck her face.

"So bad," she panted when he pulled out to let her breathe again. She looked up at him, her face and hair a complete mess now, and said in a small voice, "I need to be punished."

That is so fucking hot.

They'd never done a scene before. Maybe the make-believe at dinner was the catalyst. If so, they were definitely doing more of that.

"Come here," he groused and bent down to pick her up then tossed her on her stomach onto the bed.

He opened the jar of coconut oil and began to lube up his cock.

"I want to fuck that luscious ass of yours, Tink. Say no right now if you don't want me to."

Silence.

He spread her ass apart and dribbled some of the oil between the crack and around her star, then began probing with his finger.

"Has anyone ever fucked this delicious hole before, little one?" he asked as he breached her ring with his index finger.

"No, Sir."

Sir.

Huh, that was unexpected. And erotic as fuck. He liked the sound of it.

He dripped a little more oil down her crack, watching as it pooled at his finger, then slid a second digit in, and felt her tighten in fear.

His other hand went to her clit, and he began to rub it in circles.

"Just relax, baby. I'm just getting your ass ready so I can fuck it with my cock."

"Ohhhh," she moaned softly and lifted her ass slightly.

That's my girl.

"You want to be a good girl and let me fuck your sweet ass, don't you, baby?"

"Ye—yes, Sir," she stuttered, her voice muffled due to her face being buried in the pillow.

Her hands were clenching the sheets, her perfect ass glistening and raised in the air as he probed her with two fingers and played with her clit. It was nirvana.

His cock was leaking badly with want.

"That's my little slut," he murmured as removed his hand and lined his dick up with her ass. "Take a deep breath in, baby."

She did as he instructed and as she exhaled, he breached her ring with his cock, and she tensed up again.

"Relax, Tink," he soothed.

Even as she relaxed, she was so fucking tight, he was having a hard time moving his cock. He poured more oil down her crack and onto his dick, then proceeded to thrust slowly, letting her get used to the intrusion.

"That's it, baby. Just like that. Let me in."

Her body softened even more, and he was able to fuck her deeper.

"You are such a good slut, letting me fuck your ass like this. Do you like it, baby?"

"Yes, Sir, I do."

There was that *Sir* again.

He began to fuck her faster, grunting as he slammed his cock inside her.

"That's it. Take it. Take it all. Fuck, yeah."

She was moaning softly with her back arched just right. She was perfect.

"I'm going to come in your ass, baby," he panted, his fingers digging into her hips as held her. "Get ready…"

With a roar, he released his seed inside her. He held her tight against his hips until he finished spurting, not letting go until he'd spilled every drop. He was seeing stars, his orgasm had been so intense, and he blindly rubbed wide circles on her back until he regained his vision.

"You okay?" Jacob whispered as he slowly pulled his cock out and spread her ass cheeks to admire the cum seeping from her little star.

Fuck, that's sexy.

"Mmm hmm," she whimpered. "I think my bottom is going to be sore for a week though."

He chuckled and began to explore her wet folds until he found her clit again.

"Poor thing," he murmured. "You took my cock in your ass like such a good girl, I think you should be rewarded."

He slid a finger inside her pussy as he continued to play with her clit. "Would you like that, baby? Do you want me to play with your cunt until you come for me?"

"Yes, Sir," she panted. "I love when you make me come, Sir."

Damn! She was a natural at this.

He took his time manipulating her clit, letting her climax build slowly while leisurely continuing to finger her.

"So beautiful," he murmured as he peered down at her gleaming pussy. "Look how wet you are. You like me finger fucking you, don't you, dirty girl?"

Her pussy clamped down on his fingers, and he knew she was on the edge.

"I love it so much," she whimpered.

Jacob, still not in a hurry to have her come, picked up the pace, but only slightly.

Taren arched her back and widened her legs.

"Mmm, that's it. Spread those beautiful cunt lips open for me."

She was moaning louder, letting out mewls of desire.

"Do you want to come, baby?"

"Please. Please make me come."

With a grin, he added a second finger and started polishing her little pearl faster, and was rewarded instantly when she began to buck against his hand.

"That's it, come all over my fingers," he commanded.

She dropped her chest to the bed and began to shudder and thrash.

"Oh my god, yes!" she cried out as she continued spasming.

It was fucking sexy and his cock went from semi to hard again. He'd never be satisfied when it came to her.

She was now lying completely flat on the bed without even using a pillow, her hair sticking to her face and mascara streaked down her cheeks. She was a beautiful mess. And it was because of him.

Jacob got up and returned with a warm washcloth and gently tended to her pussy then her ass. Then he began to firmly rub her shoulders.

"Oh my god, Jake, that feels so good," she moaned into the bedspread.

No more *Sir*. He was Jake again. And he was perfectly happy about that.

In a matter of minutes, her breathing was rhythmic, letting him know she was asleep. He returned to his cabin and turned down the bed, then walked back in and scooped her up—carrying her to his room.

She woke up and rubbed her eyes, looking around confused as he deposited her on his bed.

"We got your bed pretty dirty. Let's sleep in a clean one."

"Mmmkay," she mumbled as she turned over and hugged her pillow.

He sat watching her for a long time, hardly believing she was here. But she was, and he was going to do everything in his power to keep it that way. He couldn't lose her again.

Normally, Jacob only slept a few hours a night before getting up and working. That night, after seven long years, she was finally in his arms as he fell asleep, and for the first time in a long time, he slept until morning.

Chapter Ten

Taren

She woke with a smile—she couldn't remember the last time she'd done that, and felt for him; fully expecting him not to be next to her. He'd always been an early riser.

The dirty things they'd done came flooding back to her, and her cheeks burned at the memory of how wanton and slutty she'd been. The things he'd said to her. The things *she'd* said to him. And the things he'd done to her. All those naughty, delicious things.

Her tender butt was another reminder. She'd lost her anal virginity last night, *and* she'd squirted—all in the same night. Then called him Sir! She'd been so turned on when he called her his slut, and said he was playing with her *cunt*. Then he held her tenderly all night long.

Taren realized there wasn't another man alive she could have done those things with. She would have been too ashamed, too uncomfortable. But not with Jake. She could just *be* when she was with him—whether she was feeling feisty, grumpy, slutty, happy... he loved all of her.

Her Jake....

Jake, the secret agent.

She sat up suddenly when the memory of what he'd told her at dinner surged to the forefront of her mind. Looking around, she pulled the covers to her chest, not sure what she was expecting to find. His room looked exactly like hers, except he hadn't unpacked, and his luggage was sitting open on the suitcase stand. The battered, brown leather attaché case he always traveled with was in the corner on the floor.

She heard his voice coming from the balcony and tiptoed closer to listen.

"Everything has been taken care of." *Pause.* "No, unfortunately I'm not seeing to this personally, I've got another commitment." *Pause.* "Well, I'm sorry, this one takes precedence. The best men in the business are there to help handle the situation. You'll be fine without me."

She was more important than whatever the person on the other end was talking about. *She* took precedence.

Jacob sighed loudly. "Fine. I'll be in Ensenada tomorrow. I can meet you then and go over the details there." *Pause.* "No, I can't be there sooner than that. I'm out of the country at the moment." *Pause.* "None of your goddamn business, Mason. I'll see you tomorrow." She heard a muffled thud like he'd thrown the phone onto a seat cushion, and he muttered a few expletives.

"That goddamn kid is going to be the death of me."

Kid? Does Jake have a kid?

****

"Good morning, beautiful," he greeted her with a big smile and closed his laptop when she walked onto the balcony clad only in the button-down shirt he'd worn to dinner last night. "How did you sleep?"

"Much better than the night before."

Reaching for her wrist, he tugged her into his lap. "How's the bum?" he asked with his chin on her shoulder.

"Tender."

He reached between her legs and began to caress her inner thighs, then ran his fingertip up her slit.

"How's my pussy?"

"*Your* pussy?"

"Taren," he warned. "Do you need a reminder about who this pussy belongs to?"

"No, I don't," she snapped.

That caused him to draw his hand from between her legs and wrap both around her shoulders to turn her to face him.

"What's going on?"

"Not disclosing something is the same as lying, you know."

He furrowed his brow as he cocked his head.

"What haven't I disclosed? I mean, I'm sure there's lots of things I haven't told you about, but it's not because I'm hiding anything—I just haven't gotten around to telling you about it. It hasn't even been forty-eight hours, baby. We've got the rest of our lives."

"This is something that's pretty big. You should have told me."

He looked toward the sky for a moment, like he was requesting patience from above.

"Tinkerbell, I honestly have no idea what you're talking about. What haven't I told you?"

"You have a son."

He blinked at her like she was speaking a foreign language, then repeated, "I have a son? Since when?"

"I heard you. On the phone just now. You're meeting him tomorrow."

He sat there silently for a moment, then started chuckling. Reaching for his phone, he swiped a few buttons then brought up a picture of a good-looking couple just a little older than her who appeared to be in their wedding apparel.

"If he's my son, I had him when I was about five or six."

She could feel the heat from her embarrassed cheeks.

"But you said... you said *that kid* was going to be the death of you."

"Baby girl," he said, still laughing. "I never said *my* kid. Mason may only be five years my junior, but sometimes he acts much younger. That's why I called him kid."

"Oh," she said, looking at the floor. This is what happens when she goes off half-cocked and doesn't think things through. If she'd stopped to think about it, of course it wouldn't have made sense he'd talk to his son like that.

"Maybe you need to be taught a lesson about eavesdropping."

****

Jacob

Her blue eyes flew to his, opening wide at the realization of his meaning.

"No, really, I learned my lesson. I'm very embarrassed at my mistake."

He shook his head with an empathetic smile. "Not good enough, Tink."

Lifting her off him, he stood and took her hand to lead her back inside the cabin, where he sat down on the bed.

"I'm glad you don't have any panties on," he growled as he patted his lap. "Come on."

Taren reluctantly laid her ass across his thighs, her upper body resting on her forearms supported by the bed as she looked back at him.

"Eyes forward," he demanded and began to rub her bottom with both hands. God, he loved this little ass of hers. He couldn't wait to see it pink.

She squeaked when the first blow came down on her left cheek, followed by a series of whacks to her right, then back to her left, until her ivory skin was marred a deep shade of pink.

He could smell her arousal and slipped his finger between her legs to find her pussy slick with desire.

"Naughty girl," he admonished with a grin as he delivered swats to her center. "You're not supposed to like your punishment."

She let out a muffled whimper, and he slid two fingers inside her, finger fucking her with one hand as he delivered a rain of blows to her ass with the other. The next thing he knew, her pussy was milking his fingers.

He grabbed her hair and tugged her head back. "Did you just fucking come while getting a spanking, you dirty slut?" he scolded harshly.

Although he secretly loved it. His little sprite had a kinky side. Jacob was going to love exploring this with her.

"I'm sorry, Sir!" she cried out.

"On your knees," he commanded roughly, dragging her off his lap as he stood, then undoing his pajama bottoms and tugging them down to his ankles. She was on her knees with her hands on her thighs looking up at him with her big eyes now the color of the ocean during a storm. Jacob grabbed a fistful of her hair and used it to direct her mouth to his cock, which she dutifully began to suck. He started thrusting into her throat until she made small gagging sounds, then he pulled her off his cock. She looked up at him, her eyes watery from being gagged. It was so fucking hot.

Letting go of her hair, both hands came around to frame her face under her chin, and he began to slam into her mouth like a jackhammer. She made noises from her throat as she took her face fucking like a trouper.

"Oh, yeah. That's it. Take my cock," he snarled. His balls started drawing up with his impending orgasm. He would have loved to hold off, this was so fucking hot, but she probably needed to work up a tolerance to having her throat violated.

Yanking out of her mouth, he started jerking his cock, aiming the head at her face as he unleashed his load onto her cheeks and mouth.

Her face looked absolutely tantalizing glazed with his cum, and he smiled at his handiwork. Then the little temptress put his cock back into her mouth and sucked him dry with a devilish grin.

"You are so fucking sexy," he said with a smile as he caressed the clean side of her face.

Taren popped his cock out of her mouth, still grinning. "So are you."

"Let me get you a towel, baby."

She stood up and shook her head. "I'm just going to go jump in the shower." As she walked toward her cabin, she called out over her shoulder, "Do you want to go to breakfast?"

"Yeah. I just need to finish a few things but I think I can be ready by the time you are."

"Okay."

He heard her shower turn on and smiled to himself.

Wasn't he supposed to be the one serving a penance? If this was making amends to her, he was going to spend the rest of his life atoning: happily.

Chapter Eleven

Taren

One thing she knew for sure, they were definitely compatible in bed. Because, holy hell, she'd loved every minute of their naked time together.

But as far as everything else... the jury was still out.

While she accepted his apology and explanation, wounds that are seven years deep don't just heal in two days' time. And when they did heal, they were going to leave a scar. Could she get past that?

The truth was, she didn't know. And even if she could, she wasn't sure how she felt about being in a relationship with someone whose job could put her life in danger. She wanted to have children someday; being an independent 'troubleshooting consultant' for the CIA and their allies probably didn't make him a good daddy candidate.

Sitting on the deck over breakfast, Taren watched him carefully. His smile was easy, the lines around his eyes were new, but other than that, he was her old Jake.

"How did we go three years together, and I never had a clue—not one? I feel stupid."

He sat up straighter and reached for his orange juice. "First of all, don't feel stupid." He took a sip and then continued. "I'm pretty good at what I do, but more importantly, it didn't have anything to do with our relationship—why would you have known?"

"How can you say it didn't have anything to do with our relationship, and then give it as the reason why you broke up with me?"

His eyebrows drew together and he nodded his head for a second, as if contemplating what she'd said. Finally, he looked at her and sighed. "That's a good point. You're right. But at the time, keeping that part of my life separate from you seemed easy, which I was grateful for because, honestly, I didn't have a choice in the matter. I wasn't permitted to tell you. I was trained to compartmentalize everything, including my job and my personal life. But knowing I was going to be seeing you soon was sometimes what kept me focused on getting the job done. I knew the sooner it was complete, the sooner I could get back to you."

"Were you ever unfaithful, when you were working? Did your job demand it?"

His reply was out of his mouth before she even finished the question. "Never."

"Were there times you wanted to tell me?"

"No." His answer surprised her and it must have shown on her face because he offered an explanation. "I was so fucking in love with you, Taren, I didn't want you to know; not only for your safety—and mine—but I was afraid you'd leave me if you knew. Maybe it was selfish, but I was grateful for the directive that I couldn't tell you."

She didn't know how to respond.

"And, baby, let's face it. You were twenty years old when you met me; that would have been really unfair of me to burden you with something like that when you were so young."

"You're right. I get it." And she did. Logically, anyway. Emotionally, not so much.

"I'm sorry, Tink. I wish I could sit here and tell you that if I had to do it all over again, I would have told you, but we agreed to tell each other the truth from now on, so I can't. I regret like hell how I ended things, but other than that... I don't regret a minute of our time together."

Neither did she. She'd never been happier in her life than when she'd been with Jacob, which was probably why she'd been so destroyed when things ended.

"I'm scared to love you again, Jake," she said softly, looking up at him. "I can't go through that heartache again."

"Tink, I swear—"

She held her hand up. "I want babies. Can you honestly sit here and tell me that our kids wouldn't be in danger because of your job?"

His expression was sad, and he slowly shook his head. "I can't. I promise I'd do everything in my power to keep them safe, but you're right, there would always be that possibility." He grabbed her hand. "But nothing in life is guaranteed, Taren."

"I just think..."

He put his fingertips to her mouth to keep her from finishing her thought.

"Don't make any decisions yet. We've got a whole week to get to know each other again. Maybe we'll discover we don't even like each other anymore and will be happy to go our separate ways at the end of the cruise."

Fat chance.

"Or maybe I'll be so head over heels in love with you, that I won't think straight and will follow you anywhere."

He sat back in his chair and winked at her. "That's what I'm counting on, baby."

****

Jacob

"Damn you, Jacob Preston Smith."

He smiled, both at her scolding him with the use of his full name, and at the memory of when she'd learned his middle name. He'd been lying on a blanket on the campus lawn, his head in her lap, trying to convince her to spend the night with him at his hotel for the first time instead of him staying in her dorm room until the early morning hours.

"And you promise you won't try anything?"

"Cross my heart, I'll be an absolute gentleman," he'd said, making an 'X' over his heart with his finger. "Your dorm room tends to get a little crowded; that's the only reason I'm suggesting it." That and he was tired of sharing her attention.

Okay, maaaybe him being sick of getting cock blocked by her roommate *might* have had something to do with his suggestion, but he really would be a gentleman—unless it was her idea to go further.

Not that he wasn't above helping her come to that decision. He'd flown in for two weekends in a row to be with her. Every time they were making out on her bed, her roommate would bound in, usually with people in tow, and they'd never leave.

"How do I know Jacob Smith is even your real name?"

He'd pulled out his Florida's driver's license, intending to put his thumb over everything but his photo and his name, but she snatched it from his hand and turned her body so he couldn't easily retrieve it.

"Preston!" she'd squealed. "Jacob Preston Smith. I like it." She then gasped and looked up at him, horrified. "Oh my god. *You're thirty*?" She'd said *thirty* like it was a curse word.

He'd nodded smugly as he snatched the license back. "I'm thirty. You've been dating a man a whole decade older than you—and you didn't even know it."

"What's wrong with you? Why aren't you dating women your own age?"

He'd tucked the ID in his wallet, returning the leather billfold to the back pocket of his jeans.

"I normally do date women my own age, but then a couple of weeks ago—almost in this very spot, some little blonde in a pink sundress sprinkled some fairy dust on me, and I've been smitten ever since."

It was true—the second he'd seen her, he was under her spell. He'd never felt that way before. It was like he'd been drawn to her by some invisible force.

"I've always been defenseless against your charms," she continued, bringing him back to the present.

"But I only use my charm for good, Tinkerbell," he teased.

"Your *own* good, you mean."

"Ouch, that hurts."

"Truth usually does," she grumbled under her breath and looked away.

He frowned when it dawned on him.

"You're serious."

"Yes, I'm serious! You're going to be charming all week, and even though I'll know better, I'll be right back in love with you, despite it only being to my detriment."

She might have bruised his ego a little just then. But more importantly, he'd been willing to push if he thought she just needed a gentle nudge, but if she seriously didn't want to be with him...

"I don't want to talk you into something you don't really want to do, Tink. I'll leave you alone for the rest of the cruise if you truly want that. I can get off tomorrow in Ensenada and let you enjoy your remaining time by yourself."

Her look of panic helped ease his mind, then she dropped, "Maybe that's for the best."

Well, shit. Did she just call my bluff? He honestly hadn't thought he was bluffing when he'd said he'd leave, but damn, he really didn't think she'd take him up on it.

He nodded his head with a sad smile, then stood up.

"Take care of yourself, Tinkerbell. And please don't let me being in New Orleans keep you from that job, if that's what you really want. I'm hardly ever there anyway. And I promise, even when I am, I'll leave you alone." He couldn't help but add, "If that's what you want."

"No, it's not what I want, you big stupid jerk! What I want is for you to have never left me in the first place, and for you to have a normal job, like an engineer or something, so I know I could have babies with you someday and not have to worry about someone harming them."

Jacob pulled his chair right next to hers and sat back down, then reached for her hands, gripping them tight while looking into her eyes.

"There's a lot of things you could wish for that I have the ability to make come true, unfortunately, that's not one of them. I can't go back in time, although believe me, I would if I could. Just know being without you hurt me as much as it did you. And no, our lives will never be normal—not like if I worked a traditional job. But I *promise* you, I'll do whatever it takes for you and our babies to be happy and safe."

Her eyes were filled with confusion.

"I don't know what's right, Jake."

His gut was telling him the right move here was to back off and let her decide on her own.

"I can't help you with that. Just know, I'll abide by whatever you decide."

"Can I wait and make a decision tomorrow?"

"Sure." He released her hands and stood up. "Just let me know in the morning so I know whether or not to take my luggage when I get off the ship tomorrow."

"You don't want to spend the day with me?"

This woman was going to be the death of him.

He sat back down again. "Of course I do. I just assumed you'd want to be alone so..." His bruised ego was now in charge. "I didn't charm you into doing something you didn't want to do—to your detriment."

"Don't be silly," she said with a sly grin. "You'd never do something like that. Would you?"

He cocked his head, trying to figure out what she was up to.

"Not to harm you, no. Never."

"Okay then," she stood up with a smirk, like she knew she was confusing him. "Let's go hang out at the pool."

****

Taren

She had no idea what the hell she was doing. One minute, she'd convinced herself she couldn't be with Jake, the next, she was beside herself thinking she wasn't going to see him again.

Good grief, woman. Pick one.

She knew deep down in her heart there was only one option. Regardless of the past hurt and the fearful future, the idea of not being with him when she'd been given another chance turned her stomach in knots. While the thought of being with him again? That filled her with joy.

Still. She couldn't make it *too* easy for him. Right?

Chapter Twelve

Jacob

By midday, he'd figured out she'd thought she'd given in too easily and was going to make him work for her forgiveness.

Not a problem. He'd been planning on doing that from the beginning—looking forward to it, actually.

When she took off her cover up at the pool and revealed her black bikini, his jaw almost hit the floor.

Along with every other male in viewing distance.

She was a damn knockout. She'd definitely filled out nicely over the last seven years. Her ex-husband was a fucking moron for cheating on her; instead of fucking her friends, the dumbass should have been home worshipping her body every damn night. That's what Jacob was planning on doing for the rest of his life, so, in a way, he was grateful to David Graham for not realizing what he had.

He supposed the same argument could be made about himself—except Jacob knew what he'd had, and he'd mourned it from the minute he walked out her door. There was no way in hell he was squandering this second chance with her. He'd grovel and play her game—whatever it took.

The waiter arrived with his Scotch and a fruity frozen drink with an umbrella for her.

"I didn't order that," she said as the man handed it to her.

"The gentleman did, ma'am."

Jacob shrugged. "I saw you eyeing it when the girl across the pool ordered it."

A small smile escaped as she put the straw between her lips and took a sip.

"Thank you. It's as delicious as I imagined it would be."

"Are you hungry? Do you want to get lunch poolside or something to snack on?"

She surprised him by leaning over and kissing him softly on the lips before replying, "No, not yet. But if you are, get something."

He furrowed his brow with a smirk. "What was that for?"

"For everything. The cruise, your company... I'm having fun. Are you?"

"I couldn't have scripted it any better."

She turned over onto her stomach. "Good, I'm glad. Would you mind putting some lotion on my back?"

Gee, would I mind rubbing your body sensuously? Hmm...that was a tough one. He suspected she knew what touching her body would do to him.

"You need to warm the lotion up first though," she demanded.

He smirked. She was loving her perceived power. He'd play along—for now.

"I wouldn't dream of putting cold lotion on your back, Ms. Fairchild."

She lifted her head and lowered her glasses on her nose to look at him.

"Ha ha. Very funny."

He rubbed the lotion vigorously between his hands before touching the middle of her back with it and working outward, spending a lot of time on her shoulders.

"God, Jake, that feels so good," she cooed, her body becoming more pliant with every stroke.

He worked his way down her back, then continued to her thighs. Not wanting to stop caressing her, he also lotioned her calves and arms, and anywhere else that was currently exposed to the sun.

"I love when you touch me," she murmured, sounding half-asleep.

"That makes two of us."

"You always did take such good care of me," she continued with a sigh. He could see her eyes were closed behind her glasses.

"I will again, if you'll let me."

"You'll just break my heart again."

She turned her head, like the conversation was over. Jacob wasn't a fan of being dismissed like that—especially with her parting shot that he'd break her heart again. He'd do no such thing, dammit. He ran his hands down her back again to her legs, rubbing her slit over her swimsuit discreetly as he rubbed between her thighs. She spread her legs a little wider for him; he wasn't sure if she'd done it intentionally or subconsciously.

"Mmm, that's a good girl. Spread those legs for me," he whispered in her ear as he took another subtle swipe over the fabric.

He could feel the heat generating between her legs.

"You have no idea how badly I want to bury my face between these thighs," he growled, massaging her legs in circles.

Taren turned her face back toward him and whimpered.

"Would you like that, Tink?"

"Mmm hmm," she responded; her tone higher pitched than normal.

"Me too, baby, I promise to take you back to your cabin later and do just that."

"I'm ready, now," she whispered breathlessly, eyes still closed.

He drained his Scotch and set it on the side table before standing up.

"Unfortunately, I've got to go make some calls," he said. "Do you want me to bring you back anything?"

He watched her open her eyes slowly, then look up at him with a smirk.

"You're getting me all hot and bothered and then leaving me to go work? Why am I not surprised?"

One eyebrow lifted as he warned, "Watch it, little one, or you'll be over my knee again." She bit her bottom lip, and Jacob tried to disguise his grin. "I won't be long. I've just got to get a few things ready for my meeting in Ensenada tomorrow.”

She shrugged like she didn’t care and turned over onto her back.

“I’m sure I can find someone to put more lotion on my back if you take too long.”

He surveyed the deck filled with men her age, some discreetly trying to check her out. He’d already figured out which few were going to be brave enough to approach her after he left.

“I wouldn’t advise that.”

“Jealous?”

He shook his head nonchalantly. “Nah. Territorial.”

“What’s the difference?” she scoffed.

He leaned down and growled in her ear, “Jealous is when you want something that isn’t yours. Territorial is protecting what belongs to you.”

“Who says I belong to you?” she challenged.

He wanted to respond, *I do*, but knew there was some gamesmanship going on right now.

“Fair enough. If you get a better offer, I’ll walk away and wish you well. But make sure it’s a better offer, otherwise your ass is going to be pink for trying to make me jealous.”

She dropped her glasses down her nose and glared at him.

“I thought you said you’re territorial?”

“You reminded me I don’t have a right to say that. Yet.”

"You—" she looked down and picked at her towel before glancing back at him. "You could probably say it."

He broke out into a wide smile and leaned down to kiss her below her ear.

"I'll be back before you know it."

****

Taren

She dozed off in the sun with a smile on her face. Her heart was light; although she hadn't said it out loud yet, she knew she was going to give Jake another chance. That knowledge made her happy, relieved, even.

And the sex? Oh dear god; not even in her dirtiest fantasies had she imagined it this good. There was something to be said for surrendering control to someone you trust. And she did trust him.

"Ready for another?"

She opened her eyes to see a good looking, bronzed, shirtless man holding a red slushy drink like the one Jacob had ordered for her earlier.

Taren took the offered drink and set it down on the table next to her.

"Thanks," she said with a polite smile.

"Mind if I sit?" the blond man asked as he plopped down in the chair Jacob had occupied earlier.

"Well, um, that's my…. That's my boyfriend's seat. He'll be back in a few minutes."

It felt weird calling Jake her boyfriend, but she hoped that would help move the guy along. While the *idea* of Jacob being jealous—or territorial, whatever—over her was sexy, she wasn't sure if she actually wanted to see it in action.

"I'll just keep you company until he comes back," the man said dismissively. "I'm Jeff, by the way," he said, holding his hand out, which she dutifully took.

"Taren."

"Nice to meet you, Taren. Is this your first cruise?"

"It is, actually. My boyfriend surprised me with it."

She kept talking about Jake, hoping the guy would get the hint.

"So what do you do for work?" Jeff asked.

"I'm, um, a nurse," she said nervously, looking around for Jacob. "And you?"

"I'm in software sales."

"That sounds interesting," she said politely.

She was reaching for the drink Jeff had brought her when a shadow loomed over her and Jake plucked the fruity drink from the table and replaced it with a glass of water.

"You need to hydrate, baby. You've been in the sun a long time today."

She picked up the water and took a long sip. She hadn't realized how thirsty she was.

He set the hurricane glass on a passing waiter's tray and sat down next to her on the lounger, which she had eagerly made room for him to do.

"Sorry, my calls took longer than I expected," he said before leaning down and kissing her cheek.

"I think I must have dozed off because it feels like you just left."

"That's good." He eyed Jeff, who was still sitting in Jake's seat, and offered his hand. "Jacob Smith."

"Jeff Daugherty," the blond man said, shaking Jacob's hand.

"Well, Jeff, if you'll excuse us, I need to get my girl out of the sun and back to the cabin. She's going to be red."

Taren knew exactly what he meant by that. He was going to spank her ass red.

She clenched her thighs. It had turned her on so much when he laid her across his lap earlier, much to her shock.

But, she also didn't feel like she had earned a spanking right now. She hadn't done anything wrong, and it was important to her that Jake not feel like she was deserving of punishment.

She'd happily take it when she felt she deserved it—she suspected there would be plenty of times she'd purposefully be a brat just to earn being bent over his knee.

But not now. She'd had no control over Jeff sitting down—surely Jacob had to realize that?

Taren demonstratively kissed along his jawline, then stared up lovingly into his eyes as she leaned against him. "Can we grab some food first? I'm starving."

He pecked her on the lips. "We'll get room service," he answered authoritatively.

She wanted to pout but Jeff was still sitting on the lounger next to them, watching their exchange closely. Suddenly, she was irritated with the stranger for getting her in trouble. How childish was that?

With an angry sigh, she stood and began gathering her things, silently stuffing her belongings into her big bag with conviction.

Jeff took the hint and stood up, hesitating before walking away.

"Well, hope to see you guys around. Maybe we could have drinks some night."

"Maybe," she replied.

Jake didn't respond directly, instead simply said. "Nice meeting you. Thanks for keeping Taren company after I stepped away."

She knew that was Jacob's way of letting the man know he noticed Jeff had chosen to wait until he'd left before approaching Taren.

Jeff smiled sheepishly, knowing he'd been busted. "Talk to you later," he said before quickly heading toward the bar.

"I don't deserve to be punished," she said in clipped tones as they started walking toward her cabin.

"No?" he asked with one eyebrow raised.

"Obviously you disagree. But you're wrong. I didn't ask him to sit down; I discouraged it, actually. I talked about you the whole time. I was not trying to make you jealous at all."

"Did you order the drink you were going to take a sip of?"

She cocked her head. "What?"

"Did you order the drink? Did the server deliver it or did he?"

She thought back to when Jeff had shown up.

"He brought it over."

"And you were going to drink it. Having no idea if he'd slipped something in it."

She hadn't considered that. It'd never even crossed her mind.

They arrived at her stateroom, which had been cleaned since they left earlier.

"Well, um."

"You have to take your safety seriously, Tink. Especially now. You're going to have to be aware of your surroundings, and learn how to tell people *no*. It's not all fairy dust and rainbows, baby."

"I can't believe there's more bad than good, Jake. I *refuse* to believe it."

"I love that about you, my little sprite. And I don't want you to lose that, but, baby... there are a lot of bad people in my world. You're going to have to be more cautious now. It's just the way it's going to have to be." He sat down on the bed and patted his thighs. "This will help reinforce that."

She crossed her arms and scowled at him, not moving. "No."

He cocked his head. "No?"

"I don't deserve to be spanked. Not for this. There are other ways you can *reinforce* what you've told me."

Jacob held his hand out to her, beckoning her closer. She reluctantly approached him, and he pulled her into his lap, tucking her against his chest.

"How else should I reinforce that you have to be more careful?" With a finger under her chin, he lifted her face to look at him. "I've just got you back in my life; I would lose my mind if something happened to you."

She stared into his eyes; the emotion at the thought of something happening to her on the surface as he looked back at her.

"I promise I'll be more careful," she whispered.

"You better be, Tink." He pressed his lips against hers, the kiss was raw, like he was trying to drive his point home. She had an overwhelming need to offer him comfort—she *would* be more careful. She understood how important it was to him.

Breaking the kiss, Taren slid off his lap and laid her body across it, tugging her cover up past her waist and offering her bottom to him.

Chapter Thirteen

Jacob

His breath caught in his chest when she draped herself across his lap in submission. He ran his hands in wide circles across her round globes, appreciating just how luscious her ass felt in his palms.

He knew she thought he'd developed a spanking fetish in the seven years they'd been separated; but that wasn't the case. Sure he'd smacked a few asses while fucking a girl doggie style, but he'd never wanted a woman's submission the way he wanted Taren's. He'd never asked a woman to surrender control to him like he was expecting Tink to do.

Like he *needed* her to do.

That she was giving it to him so freely was not something he was taking lightly.

"You have to be more careful, little one," he said then rained down six blows to her cheeks over her swimsuit bottoms.

Rubbing tenderly where he'd just spanked, he said in a low voice, "Tell men *no*, because if you don't, then your next punishment is going to be with a belt."

Jacob alternated ten more slaps then yanked her bottoms down to expose her skin and found her ass red. His dick was already hard, but seeing her beautiful skin reflecting his handiwork made it even harder.

He knew he was going to find her soaked before he even slid his finger down her slit. She spread her legs wider when he did, causing him to chuckle out loud even as he removed the restriction of how far she could spread by removing her bikini bottoms and tossing them aside.

"Naughty girl. You're not supposed to like this so much."

That was a lie. He loved that it turned her on.

He slapped her center, and she involuntarily moaned out loud, trying to muffle the sound into the bedspread.

"There are bad people in my world, Tink. You have to promise to be vigilant and pay attention."

He spanked her pussy again and felt her quiver, like she was trying to pull him inside, and he bit back a groan.

"I can't lose you again, baby," he growled as he slid two digits into her heat and began to slowly finger fuck her.

He spanked her ass, *hard*, with one slap, causing her to jump then fist the bedding.

"Promise me!" he barked, then spanked her again, all while fingering her soaked cunt.

"I promise," she panted.

He began to fuck her faster as he delivered a succession of smacks to her fleshy bottom.

"What are you going to say to men you who offer you a drink?"

"No," she half-moaned, half gasped, and lifted her ass higher.

While he was debating the merits of orgasm denial to drive his point home, he felt her entire body go rigid. He needed to make a decision *now* before she climaxed.

Slowing his fingers to a halt, he asked, "Do you think I should let you come? After you almost took a sip of a drink that could have had something slipped into it?"

"I'm sorry, Sir," she cried, pressing against his hand as if trying to coax him into resuming his ministrations. "I promise it won't happen again."

When he didn't move to touch her again, she begged, "Please, Sir."

The *Sir* and the begging were too much for him to take, and he quickly lifted her off his lap and began to undo his pants. He needed to be inside her *now*.

"Get on your hand and knees," he commanded as he dropped his slacks and boxer briefs to the floor.

With one swift motion, Jacob was balls deep inside her and he bit out, "Fuuuuck," between clenched teeth. Reaching around with one hand, he swatted her pussy as he drove into her hard. Feeling her body tense, he polished her clit in rhythm with his thrusts, and within seconds, she was coming undone underneath him, her back arching as she moaned out loudly—she was a goddamn sex goddess.

The visual of her as she came, along with her tight pussy quaking around his cock, was his undoing, and with a grunt, he held her hips tight as he came deep inside her. This seemed to spark another orgasm from her, either that or her climax was lasting an unusually long time. Either way, it was hot as hell, and his ego loved it, so he continued thrusting inside her until she went still and collapsed her entire body onto the bed.

He sat back on his heels and watched his cum seep out of her. If he lived to be one hundred, he would never tire of that sight. It was the ultimate way to brand her as his.

And make no mistake, Taren Scarlett Fairchild was *his*. He was never letting her go again.

****

Taren

They took a nap after their sexscapade. Well, she did anyway. She suspected he'd only lain with her until he knew she was asleep, then he got up and did more work. He'd been really good about being present with her; not checking his phone every five minutes like David always had—even while wooing her. But Jake also hardly slept, and Taren knew he was working while she was sleeping.

Luckily for him, she was a big fan of naps and sleep in general.

Taking a full body stretch, she smiled when she realized she was still naked, then slowly sat up and looked around for something to put on. His button down was lying on top of his open suitcase, so she slipped it on before heading out to the balcony where she heard his voice.

The sun was going down, and he smiled when he looked up and saw her approaching him cautiously—unsure if it was okay for her to be out there with him while he was on the phone.

He reached for her wrist and tugged her on his lap, effectively answering her unspoken question.

"Everything is set, Mason. If you question me one more time, my rate is going to double. I'm already pissed that you're interrupting my vacation with this meeting tomorrow. Don't push it."

He kissed her hair and stroked her back as he listened to the man on the other end of the phone.

"Noon, tomorrow. The Guzman estate. I only have an hour, so don't be late."

Without another word, he hung up and set the phone down on the table next to them, then wrapped both arms around her, continuing to stroke her back with his chin on her shoulder.

"Hi, baby. You must be hungry?"

"Starving."

"Do you want to go to the dining room or order room service?"

Their meal at the restaurant last night had been delicious, but she was really comfy in just his shirt and didn't feel like getting dressed and ready to go out.

"Eating dinner in bed sounds perfect," she said, turning her body so she could stroke his cheek.

"Your wish is my command, little one."

Her old Jake had always doted on her; it was something she'd missed so much—especially because David never did after they were engaged. She didn't think Jake would ever stop cherishing her—he seemed hardwired to care for her. The 'new' Jacob was even more attentive than she remembered.

And the 'new' Jacob in bed? *Oh. My. God.*

"So, when we were together before... did you ever want to spank me then?"

She felt him chuckle.

"Where did that come from? Maybe we should order dinner first before we start reminiscing."

Her question *was* kind of out of the blue, but it was something she'd been wondering ever since he first smacked her bottom, and she orgasmed all over his fingers because of it.

"Are you avoiding the question?"

He softly kissed her neck then let his hands wander to caress her inner thighs. If this was a diversion tactic of his, it wasn't going to work.

Okay, maybe for just a minute or two.

"I'll take that as a *yes*, you're avoiding the question," she murmured as she tilted her head to allow him better access to her neck.

Jake stopped kissing her and said with a laugh, "Not avoiding the question. You're just too tempting when you're sitting here on my lap." He moved his hands under her butt and lifted her off him.

"Let's order dinner and we can talk while we wait for it to get here."

****

They ordered, and he was standing at the credenza, pouring a glass of single malt Scotch when he said, "To answer your earlier question, no I didn't have a desire to spank you seven years ago."

Her heart sunk; that meant he'd acquired this interest with someone else. She'd had two sex partners in her life; how could she compete with someone who'd help him develop this kink?

"Oh," was all she could think to respond.

He turned around and looked at her intently. So intently she began to fidget from her seat on the couch.

"You've always given me your submission, Tink—probably without even realizing it. When you were twenty-three, you looked at me like I hung the moon; I didn't need anything else from you. But the older you? The one who's seen more of life and is no longer impressed that I can speak five languages and realizes that I did not hang the moon? You've experienced my biggest mistakes first hand—you know I'm fallible, and I want your submission now more than ever. I fucking crave it. Spanking you just feels natural."

It felt natural to her too. Still, she had her hang ups with him spanking previous lovers.

"I know it's none of my business, but when did you start wanting women's submission? Before you met me, when you were with women your age—did you discipline them?"

He took a long pull of his drink as he contemplated her question.

"Without getting into specifics, I'm a dominant lover—yes. I have to be in charge. But, Tink, you're the only woman I've asked to submit to me; you're the only woman whose total submission I've wanted. Anyone else I was with... well, to put it bluntly, she was satisfying a biological urge. Nothing more. You... you're so much more to me."

She was having a hard time processing her feelings. Shouldn't she feel ashamed and that what he was telling her was wrong? How could his saying she was the only girl he'd ever wanted to discipline make her feel special? What fucking universe was she in right now? She was a feminist for chrissake—and here she was *wanting* to be submissive to this man?

The funny thing was, she'd never felt more powerful than when surrendering to him. Maybe it was because she was *giving* it to him, rather than him taking it? She knew she could take it back at any time. Relinquishing control to Jake was nothing like being with David. Her husband's power over her had been for his benefit, not hers. He hadn't had her best interest at heart; in fact, anytime she attempted to exert control over her own life or tried to have a say in their marriage, he'd felt threatened.

Not Jake.

She knew even though she'd offered him her submission, he liked her sass. Wanted it. She felt more equality with Jacob, even as she was bent over his knee, than she ever had with David.

Just then there was a knock on the door, with Manuel announcing, "Room service!"

Jacob's eyes searched hers—an unspoken question evident on his face, and she realized she hadn't responded to what he'd just shared.

Chapter Fourteen

Jacob

He opened the door and Manuel wheeled the cart with their dinners in.

"Would you like me to set up on the balcony or at the table?" he asked.

Jacob looked at Taren with raised eyebrows.

"On the balcony, please," she said with a polite smile as she pinched the terrycloth material closed at her chest. She had dashed to the bathroom when she heard the door knock and came out wearing the fluffy robe she'd gotten from the spa just as he let Manuel in.

After the steward set their dishes out and lit a fake candle, Jake showed him to the door, handing the man a twenty on his way out, then came back and promptly untied her robe and pulled it off her, letting it drop in a heap on the ground. She looked sexy as fuck in only his shirt.

He shut the cabin lights off and escorted her to the balcony. Pulling her chair out for her to slide onto, he glanced down at the gap in the shirt to admire her braless tits in the glow of the LED candlelight. She really had gotten better with age.

Unable to help himself, he reached down to caress a soft mound of her creamy flesh. She looked at him with a knowing smile, but didn't say anything.

"Sorry, couldn't resist," he murmured as he removed his hand and took a seat.

They had been interrupted after his admission that he felt the need to dominate her, and he was a little worried about what she was thinking. Not that he was worried she didn't like it—her body had already told him otherwise, but saying the words out loud was different.

They removed the metallic domes covering their plates at the same time; the smell of their dinners hitting his olfactory system and making his stomach growl.

"This looks amazing," she said as she laid the napkin across her lap. "I can't believe how delicious the food is here."

"Haven't you been on a cruise before?"

She shook her head. "I haven't really traveled very much."

"Oh, baby, I'm going to love showing you the world." And it was going to be in style—because that's what she deserved, and frankly, he could afford it.

After taking a bite of her vegetable lasagna, she swallowed and smiled. "I think I'll love that, too."

Well, that was good news.

"So, I couldn't tell what you were thinking before dinner got here," he said nonchalantly as he cut his salmon.

"I think..." she said as she pushed her food around on her plate, not looking at him. Finally, she shyly glanced up. "I think I like our dynamic."

That made him smile. "Yeah?"

"Yeah. It makes me feel powerful, if that makes any sense."

"I hope so, baby. I always want you to feel like you have control, but also feel comfortable giving it to me because you know I'll always take care of you."

She pressed her lips together, her eyes brimming with tears. *Fuck! What did I do?*

"I do know that," she whispered. "I've missed you so much. I've been pinching myself wondering if you're really here."

He was kneeling at her side before the first tear fell, wiping her eyes as they did.

"I am here, Tink. For good—I'm not going anywhere. I promise. It's you and me, baby girl. Forever."

She wrapped her arms around his neck and her tiny body began to wrack with sobs. He lifted her out of her chair and walked back into the dark cabin, sitting down on the couch with her in his arms. Rocking her gently, he just held her while she cried, but his heart was breaking over how much pain he'd put her through.

"I'm so sorry, baby," he murmured against her hair. His shirt was wet against his skin from her tears.

He'd been naïve thinking all was forgiven, and they'd just move forward with their happily ever after. It was going to take a long time for her to heal and completely trust him again—he realized that now. He was going to have to keep showing her how sorry he was and proving that he would never leave her again.

"Your heart's safe with me, Taren. I promise.

****

Taren

She had no idea where the tears had come from, but it'd been a rollercoaster of a day as far as her emotions were concerned. Looking at Jacob as he told he was going to show her the world, she thought about how much fun that would be, then panic set in when she thought back to when he'd pulled the rug out from under her. But he was here *now,* and he swore he wasn't going anywhere—plus with all the secrets he'd told her, she knew in her heart she could believe him. All that, on top of their discussion about him wanting her submission... it had all become overwhelming.

The crying felt cathartic, especially since Jake simply held her as she did, but it also left her physically drained.

She heard his stomach rumbling and realized she was still hungry, too.

"I'm so sorry we hardly ate any dinner. Now it's cold."

He reached over and picked up the phone receiver on the table next to the couch and started dialing.

"Hi, this is Cabin 1136. Can you send a repeat of our last order, but with dessert this time?"

Pause. She could see the features of his face in the moonlight shining through the window. God, he was beautiful.

"Whatever you have is fine. Pie, cake, ice cream... send it all. Thanks."

He hung up, and she giggled as she asked, "Send all the desserts?"

Taren felt him shrug. "Dessert makes everything better."

She put her head back on his shoulder. "So do you."

His strong arms came back around her, and he continued to hold her in the dark, quiet room, his cheek resting on her head as his fingertips traced up and down her spine. If not for the hunger pangs in her tummy, she would have been content to sit there all night nestled against his chest.

The knock on the door came sooner than she expected, and she slid off his lap.

"I'm going to go wait in your cabin. I don't want anyone to see me like this."

She was sure she was a mess from bawling. Her eyes felt puffy, and she was certain her skin was splotchy.

He nodded. "I'll let you know when he's left."

Jake called her back less than three minutes later; their dinner set up in the suite this time at the table that was bigger than the one on the balcony. In addition to the two dinners, there was a variety of desserts—ranging from ice cream sundaes to pies, cakes, and tarts, sitting on the table.

"Wow, that makes me want to have dessert first," she crooned as she inched her chair closer to her plate.

"You're a grown woman—do what you want."

"I'm debating between having warm lasagna instead of hot, or a semi-melted sundae."

"Go for the ice cream," he said with a smirk as he took a spoonful himself. "It's really good. Besides, you're on vacation—you *should* have dessert first."

Taren looked at the smorgasbord in front of her and shook her head in amazement.

"Thank you," she gestured to the food, then to her surroundings. "For all of this. You've been incredibly generous. I really appreciate it. I'll buy this dinner, since it's my fault our first one was ruined."

He lifted the silver covering on his entrée, the steam rising from the bed of rice next to his salmon.

"I appreciate the offer, but it's not happening," he said before taking a bite. "And it wasn't your fault. You needed to let that out."

Taren nodded as she scooped hot fudge and vanilla ice cream from the goblet and took a bite. She felt so decadent having dessert first.

"Wanna tell me what that was all about?" he asked quietly, his expression sober as he continued eating his meal.

She took another bite of sundae—bigger this time as she decided how to respond.

"I think it finally caught up with my brain that you're really back in my life. I guess I'm so used to thinking about you with mixed emotions, I just couldn't process everything."

"Mixed emotions? You mean sometimes you didn't hate me?"

"I never hated you, Jake. You obliterated my heart, and I had no idea why, so I was devastated for a long time. But I eventually was able to look back on our time together with fondness. You taught me a lot about life, and I really was happy when I was with you. Deliriously, ridiculously happy."

He smiled and said, "Me, too, Tink. I'll make you happy like that again, I promise."

She gave him a sad smile. "I think I'm afraid to let myself believe that." He opened his mouth to protest, but she cut him off. "I believe you when you say you're not going anywhere. You've told me some pretty heavy stuff that I don't think you'd share with me if you weren't serious. But I think there's a tiny piece of my soul that wants to protect me from ever experiencing that pain again. Finding out my *husband* was *cheating* on me, didn't hurt half as bad as the day you broke up with me. I really don't think I would survive you leaving me again, Jake."

He set his silverware down and looked at her thoughtfully, then slid to his knee at her side and took her hand.

"Let's get married."

Chapter Fifteen

Jacob

"What?! Are you crazy? I just got a divorce two weeks ago—I can't get engaged already." Taren exclaimed.

"Says who?" he asked with a furrowed brow as he sat back in his seat.

"Says me!" She took another bite of her dessert, not looking at him. "Why would you ask me that now?"

"Because I love you, and I do want to marry you. I can't think of how else I can ease your mind that I'm here forever other than to make you my wife."

"That's not a very good reason to ask someone to marry you. Besides, it's too soon. I can't get engaged after just getting divorced."

"I think it's a damn good reason. And who said anything about being engaged? I want to marry you, not be engaged to you."

"Oh my god, that's even worse!"

He scowled. "This isn't exactly how I envisioned the reaction to my proposal, you know."

She scraped the side of the sundae glass with her spoon.

"If I thought that was a planned proposal that you'd given serious consideration to, I would probably be a little kinder with my rejection of it."

The corner of his mouth lifted. "I think you're missing the point."

"Tell you what, ask me again in a year. If we're still together then, I think you'll get a more favorable response."

"We *will* be together in a year, and I'm not waiting that long to marry you, Taren."

Her eyes grew big as she swallowed the last of her ice cream. "You're not?" she squeaked.

"No."

She narrowed her eyes at him like she was mustering up some sass.

"I'm pretty sure I have a say in whether or not I get married again."

He watched as she struggled between choosing to eat her entrée or a piece of blueberry pie and tried not to smile. She'd always had a sweet tooth. She finally lifted the silver cloche from her main course and set it aside so she could start on the lasagna.

"You're right, you do. But, you'll say yes," he said confidently, laying his napkin back across lap to finish his dinner.

She looked over at him with pursed lips. "You're probably right."

That caused him to burst out laughing. "Gee, don't sound so happy about that prospect."

"It's just too soon to even consider."

Jacob shrugged. "I don't think so."

"We can agree to disagree."

"Okay, how about this? Just between you and me—we're getting married in six months. We don't have to announce it to the world; it's just an understanding between us. Wherever you want, with whomever you want there to witness it, big or small... I don't care. But it's happening in six months. Or sooner, preferably sooner. Cost is not an object."

"And that's another thing that's going to take some getting used to," she said. He noticed she didn't object to marrying him.

"What is? Not having to worry about money?"

"Yeah. Well, *you* having money. I remember only going out for pizza if we had a coupon."

He smiled at the memory. "Those were fun times. But, I'll be honest, I had more money back then than you thought."

She cocked her head. "You did? Why didn't you tell me? Not that it would have mattered as far as how I felt about you, but why did you feel the need to keep it a secret?"

"I don't think I was keeping it a secret; you made certain assumptions about what I could afford because I was flying in to see you all the time—I simply never corrected you."

"Well, I felt bad that you spent so much money on airfare and hotels."

He leaned across the table and kissed her gently on the lips as her eyes closed.

"There was nothing I'd have rather spent my money on than coming to see you, but I'm sorry you felt bad. I'll make it up to you. I promise."

She opened her eyes as he sat back in his seat. "You've got a lot to make up for," she grumbled while cutting her lasagna.

"Good thing I've got the next fifty or so years then," he said, trying to give her his best charming grin.

"I hate how easily I turn to mush with you."

"You do? Because, I love it."

She shook her head. "I don't know if I'm up for this adventure with you."

"You're up for it, you're still young," he said with a wink. "Your life will never be boring, Tinkerbell. I can guarantee that."

"That's what I'm afraid of. I like boring."

Shit, he hadn't thought about that—although he probably should have. He knew she liked low-key.

"Okay. Fair enough. You know how some people schedule vacations? Well, we'll schedule our boring times."

"You really do have an answer for everything."

Jacob reached over with his fork and cut a piece of the pie she'd been admiring, and popped it in his mouth with a grin.

"Most of the time. It's why—"

"Yeah, yeah, I know," she interrupted as she moved the pie closer to her and out of his reach. "It's why they pay you the big bucks."

She was obviously not impressed.

Chapter Sixteen

Taren

Jake was moving at light speed, and she wasn't sure how to feel about it.

Part of her understood it—maybe even appreciated it; he was trying to make up for lost time, show her he was committed. But part of her was still trying to fathom how she'd ended up here.

Three days ago, she was a fresh divorcee who hadn't had sex in almost seven months, going on a cruise paid for by a mystery sponsor, and considering a job offer from a hospital in New Orleans. And she hadn't heard from Jacob Preston Smith in over seven years after he'd shattered her heart into a million pieces.

Ever since the ship had left port, she'd had the most amazing sex in her life with the man she thought she'd never see again—the man she knew she would forever consider the love of her life. Oh, and he was a former spy and richer than sin, and he was the benefactor of her vacation and the reason she'd gotten her current job and the job offer in New Orleans.

Lying in his arms in the middle of the night, she was happy. Happier than she'd been in a really long time. It was when she was alone and *thinking* that things got muddled. She had a feeling she was going to have a lot of time for that when they arrived in Ensenada in the morning.

She certainly wasn't expecting him to say at breakfast, "Do you need to go back to the room for your passport? You'll need it when we disembark."

"Wait. We're getting off together?"

His forehead wrinkled in confusion. "Of course we are. What did you think?"

"I just assumed I'd get off alone and walk around the shops, maybe take a tour, while you did whatever it is you're doing today."

"My business this afternoon is going to take no more than an hour. Maybe while I'm doing that you can take an excursion to *La Bufadora*, but I was planning on spending the day with you in Ensenada. It's an interesting city; I'd love to show you around."

"*La Bufadora*?"

"The Blowhole. It's a marine geyser—one of only three in the world. Your sightseeing should take longer than my meeting."

"Oh. That sounds interesting, I guess."

It'd be something to do at least while he met Mason at the Guzman estate. She wasn't going to tell him she knew the details of his business today; she'd already been spanked once for eavesdropping. While technically, this would be for that same offense, Taren wasn't sure Jake would see punishing her again as double jeopardy, so she was going to feign ignorance about where he was going today, just in case he wouldn't.

"I do need to go back to my cabin to get my purse and passport, and maybe change into tennis shoes if I'm going to be walking a lot."

He was dressed in black suit pants, black wingtip dress shoes, and a cornflower blue button down shirt open at the collar with a black suit jacket. She was having a hard time imagining they'd be walking very much with him dressed like that, but she assumed on the trip to *La Bufadora*, she'd probably have to cover some distance. Probably best not to attempt it in the flip flops she currently had on.

She was actually ready to go before Jacob, and waited patiently for him at her balcony table, reading a Misty Malloy novel on her Kindle while he talked on the phone in his cabin suite. She quickly became engrossed in the story and lost track of time, so when he finally appeared in the doorway, apologizing for taking so long, she had no idea what that really meant.

"Are you ready?" he asked.

She reluctantly closed her Kindle cover and stood. *I'll get back to Misty's dragon shifters soon enough*, she soothed her inner book nerd as she gathered her purse. It was tempting to toss the Kindle in her bag, but she knew better—her nose would be back in it with any spare second, and she'd probably miss her tour bus or something.

"Here," he said, handing her a cell phone. "Put this in your purse, for emergencies. My number is programmed in it."

Her personal cell had been turned off since before they left San Diego. She didn't have an international plan, and the cruise literature warned her about possibly being charged astronomical roaming fees if her phone picked up a signal. She was on a budget; she couldn't afford that.

"Thanks," she said, taking the phone. It did make her feel better knowing she could reach him if she needed to.

They stepped out the cabin door and interlaced their fingers like old times.

"You look very cute today. That's a pretty dress."

She'd chosen a high-waisted teal dress that flared at the skirt above her knee with a pattern of big fuchsia flowers. It could be paired with heels, sandals, or Keds—depending on the look she was going for. Today, she was going for the 'preppy tourist' look.

"Thanks," she said, happy that he noticed.

"It reminds me of the first time I met you."

"When you said I was sprinkling fairy dust all over Tulane's pedestrian mall."

"Today, you can sprinkle it all over Ensenada." He grinned, and with his hand on her back, directed her down the gangway to the long concrete pier and past the customs gate where they'd have to pass through on their return to the ship.

She took the big sunglasses out of her multi-colored, straw bag and put them on as they stood in the taxi cab line.

A tinted out black luxury sedan slowly rolled up. She wouldn't have thought much about it until she felt Jake's body language shift. The back window rolled down and a cute blond man hung out the side with a shit-eating grin.

"Hey, you sexy beast, need a lift?"

Jacob sighed; a scowl on his face as he muttered under his breath, "Goddammit. I should have known." Leaning down slightly, he quietly said, "Wait here."

****

Jacob

Sonofabitch, that little asshole found me. His next thought was, *Why?*

Resting his forearms on the rear window of the car, he growled, "What are you doing here, Mason?"

Mason ignored his question and looked around Jacob at his companion, who was waiting patiently after stepping out of the taxi line.

"That's Taren, isn't it? Please tell me that's her."

Jacob refused to answer, just stared at the younger man with annoyance.

Undeterred, Mason shouted, "Taren!" and of course, she looked.

"I knew it!" he said victoriously, giving Jacob the same grin he had when he initially rolled the window down.

"What do you want, Mason? I told you I'd meet you at Dante and Bella's at noon."

"I just wanted to see if my hunch was right. Turns out, I still got it." He made a show of looking at Taren again. "She's adorable. Not at all what I envisioned your type to be, though."

"Fuck. Off," Jacob said through gritted teeth, then looked back and smiled at his pretty, blonde future wife.

"You might as well accept my ride and introduce me, otherwise, I'm just going to follow you around all morning and introduce myself."

Goddamn punk.

Jacob closed his eyes in exasperation, pinching the bridge of his nose as he took a cleansing breath in.

"If you weren't already dead, I'd kill you," he grumbled, referring to the agency listing the young agent as deceased. For all the CIA knew, Mason was dead—they'd sent him on a suicide mission and not bothered to retrieve him when shit went sideways. Jacob had been the one to extract him from the Middle East when he learned Mason was still alive. "But keep it up, and I might make it official."

Mason paid no mind to the older man's grumblings. He'd changed since leaving the agency and getting married. Relaxed. It suited him.

He'd also gotten a lot more flippant. "Call her over here!" Apparently Jacob didn't move fast enough for the younger man because he began yelling like he was catcalling her.

"Hey! Taren! Pretty blonde American lady! Come here!"

"Why don't you draw a little more attention to us, dickhead?"

Jacob turned back and saw Tink watching them, unsure of how to proceed. He gestured with his head for her to come over.

"Does she know?" Mason asked quietly as she started walking toward them.

"For the most part. You don't need to provide any details."

She was a few feet away when Jacob gave her a bright smile and held his hand out.

"Here's my girl."

She took his hand, and he drew her next to him, his arm going around her waist.

"Taren, *this* is Mason."

A slow smile crept across her face, and she held out her hand. "Nice to meet you. I've heard a lot about you."

Ugh. Not what Mason's ego needed to hear.

"He talks about me?" The younger man's eyebrows rose. "It's all lies, I assure you."

"Oh," she glanced up at Jacob, and he caught the slight turn of her mouth. "Jake said you were like the son he never had."

"I never said that!" Jacob blustered the same time Mason asked with an excited smile, "He said that? I knew he loved me."

Letting her meet anyone was such a mistake—especially Mason. Although, there weren't many others he'd even consider allowing it to happen with. Hardly anyone in their business even knew what he looked like, and of those who did—there were only a select few he trusted enough to know she existed. Mason was one, Bella was another.

The car door came open as the younger man said, "Come on, I'll show you around town before we go to Dante and Bella's for lunch."

Jacob knew it was pointless to argue right now—but she was *not* going to the Guzman estate.

Chapter Seventeen

Taren

Mason was adorable—he had a dimple in his cheek when he smiled, along with blue eyes that twinkled with mischief.

The ride into town was brief, but he peppered her with as many questions as he could fit in on the way.

"Where did you guys meet?"

"None of your business," Jacob answered, even though the question was clearly directed at Taren.

"Do you think you'll do the long distance thing, or are you planning on moving in together? Personally, I would recommend getting married."

Jacob didn't respond to his question, just glared at the man—who grinned in return. Taren suspected the cute blond man was purposefully trying to get under Jake's skin, and it appeared to be working—which surprised her. He was always cool and composed about everything. Well, about everything *except* her, it seemed.

"We haven't figured that out yet," she said to be polite.

"Reagan and I better be invited to the wedding," Mason said as they piled out of the black car and started walking along the shops and vendors.

"Why? I wasn't invited to yours," Jacob shot back, pausing to sidestep and shake his head at a vendor trying to get them to come inside his store.

"I already told you—it was spur of the moment and only our immediate family was there."

"Do you really think we're going to have a big wedding, Mason? Think about it."

Jacob turned to her with a questioning look and reached for her hand. "That's okay, isn't it?"

"I thought you said I could have as big a wedding as I wanted?" she teased.

He bit the side of his cheek and frowned. "I did say that, didn't I?"

"So you have talked about getting married! That's awesome! I'm available to be a groomsman, if you need me," Mason said with a grin.

Taren's smile was polite. "I think we will probably elope to somewhere warm if we actually do tie the knot someday. Just the two of us."

"Aw, you'll still need a witness! My wife and I would love to be there. By the way, I'm going by Edward O'Connor these days."

"Ah, yes. *Chef* O'Connor if my sources are to be believed."

"You're keeping tabs on me?" the younger man asked with a smile. "I'm so freaking flattered!"

Jacob rolled his eyes and shook his head, but then, as if in spite of himself, asked, "How's the baby?"

Mason/Edward's face lit up like the Christmas tree at Rockefeller Center. "She's perfect and brilliant and beautiful," he said as he took out his phone and started scrolling before showing them pictures of a beautiful little girl about six months old.

"She looks just like you," Taren remarked.

"You think so? I think she looks like her mama."

Jacob studied the picture, then the other man before weighing in.

"She has Reagan's eyes, but I can definitely tell she's your daughter."

The blond studied his daughter's face on his screen for a moment longer before putting his phone away.

"Second best day of my life—the day she was born."

She found herself asking, "And the first?"

"The day Reagan married me, of course."

"Of course," she said with a teasing tone.

"I can't wait to introduce you," Mason/Edward said.

"Not happening," Jacob said, and he took her hand and began to walk briskly down the sidewalk, away from the younger man.

Edward jogged to catch up.

"Come on. Everyone will want to meet her…"

"Damn it, I said no. It's not safe," Jacob interrupted.

"What are you talking about, *not safe*? The estate is probably the safest place she could be this afternoon. Everyone who's going to be there owes you a debt of some kind or another. You know that."

"You, of all people, know that even the estate is vulnerable."

A scowl formed on Edward's brow.

"Low blow, man."

Jake released her hand and tugged on Edward's elbow, pulling him a few yards away. She could still hear their conversation.

"I don't want her anywhere near my business. I would think you'd understand that better than anyone." Jacob snarled.

"I understand better than anyone that *that* is impossible."

"Bullshit. I did it for three years."

"And how'd that work out for ya?"

Oh, Taren *definitely* liked Edward. Judging by the steam practically coming out of his ears, it was safe to say to say, *Jacob, not so much.*

She approached the men and sidled up next to Jacob; entwining her hand with his.

"I think it will be okay, baby," she whispered as she looked up at him.

He stared down at her and his features visibly softened before he leaned over and kissed her forehead.

"You're going to miss your tour, then," he said, like the enticement of *La Bufadora* was enough to keep her from agreeing to go to lunch.

"You can show me the blowhole some other time. But do we have time for me to buy some souvenirs?"

"Plenty of time," Edward chimed in. He was met with Jacob's icy glare as they started toward some shops across the street that had looked appealing to Taren.

"My rate just went up," Jake grumbled as he stepped off the curb.

Even grumpy, he was sexy.

****

Jacob

Fuck. Fuck. Fuck.

He did not know how to maneuver this new territory. Not only did Taren now know what he did for a living, she was about to meet some of the people he did business with. Not at all what he had planned for the day. When things didn't go according to his plan, it made him really uneasy, which was why he made sure it didn't happen very often.

Tink sensed it, too, because she made sure to stay close to him in the shops and hold his hand or touch his arm as often as possible.

"I can still go on the tour. I don't mind," she'd said quietly when they were away from the CIA agent formerly known as Mason.

He wouldn't put it past Edward to hunt her down on the Punta Banda Peninsula where the underground geyser was located—about an hour south of Ensenada.

"At this point, baby, I think it's safer if you stay with me."

Not that he was worried anyone would hurt her today. The younger man had a point earlier—everyone at today's meeting owed him a debt of some sort or another. Jacob liked it that way—people owing him; he made sure it was never the other way around. It made doing his job so much easier when people were indebted to him.

What he was concerned with now was the appearance that he was worried about her. That would be leverage should anyone start to feel wily toward him. He knew Edward, Dante, and Bella weren't a threat, but as for the rest of the players, he wasn't so sure.

"I'm going to kick your ass," he snarled at the younger man as they started walking back toward the car. Tinkerbell was up ahead, negotiating with a street vendor over magnets or some other tchotchke shit.

"What? Why?"

"She needs to stay hidden when the others get there. Do you understand me, *Edward*? No one—and I mean *no one*, is to know about her."

"Well, that's going to be kind of hard since Reagan, Bella, and Dante know that's why I came into town. To see if she was with you and bring her back."

"I'd already taken into account that you probably told your family, which is still bullshit, by the way. If you were anyone else, I'd have you killed—just so you know."

"Well, good thing you love me and think of me as the son you never had," Edward said with a grin, completely unaffected by the threat on his life. "Let's go have lunch with my wife and her family before the others arrive. Oh, John knows, too."

Of course he did.

Exasperated, Jacob left Edward and approached his little sprite, haggling with the man behind the table like it was her job.

"How about three for eight?" she asked.

The man acted like it pained him to be agreeing to such a price, but he accepted it and began wrapping up her purchases in newspaper.

She looked over at Jacob with a victorious smile, like she'd just negotiated a multi-million-dollar merger instead of the sale of three ceramic refrigerator magnets. He couldn't help but smile back at her.

Looking at her innocent, naïve face, he felt a pang of guilt over what he was about to subject her to. She was going to be introduced into his world, and he hated it. The agency's rules had been in place for a reason—there was definitely something to be said for compartmentalizing your life and not letting the two mix. He'd sold his soul to the devil, not hers. She was too pure for this shit.

She cocked her head and looked at him, still smiling broadly. "What?"

He forced the smile to return to his face, and he slipped his arm around and kissed her hair.

"Nothing. I just love you is all."

The weathered man behind the table of souvenirs handed her the black, plastic bag with her purchases inside, and wished them a nice day in English with a heavy Mexican accent.

"You too," she called cheerfully as they walked away—sprinkling her fucking fairy dust as she went. She was practically skipping.

He tugged her closer and said in a low voice, "At lunch today, I want you to be vague about every aspect of your life; do you understand me? No details—even when they're super charming and fawning all over you. You give them a made up last name, if they ask."

"How about Johnson? We probably should have our stories match, in case you're asked."

"Well, I'll straight up tell them it's none of their fucking business, but I suspect you wouldn't be so blunt."

"Can I share that I'm a nurse?"

He thought about it for a minute.

"Okay, but nothing specific, like your specialty or where you work. Not even the city, Tinkerbell. If they press, put it on me and tell them I forbade you from saying anything."

"This is making me really nervous, now. I don't want to screw anything up accidentally."

"You'll be fine. I'm betting it will be just you and Edward's wife, Reagan, anyway once the meeting starts. Just ask her about their restaurant and their baby—that should keep her talking for at least an hour. I don't plan on this taking longer than that."

The deal Jacob had helped Edward with in Colombia was coming back to bite them all in the ass, but especially the Sinaloa cartel as the Colombian cartel sought revenge for their interference.

A small crew of CIA rebels—including Edward, and assisted by Jacob, had gone in and rescued Edward's brother, Marcus, who was also a former agent. He'd been taken hostage in Cartagena while trying to break up an international sex slavery ring. Unfortunately, the agency pulled out before they were done, but he'd fallen in love with one of the women being sold, so he wasn't willing to leave without her. It'd created a whole clusterfuck, involving Edward kidnapping Reagan to lure her sister, Bella out of retirement and bring her Sinaloa mafia husband's resources with her—falling in love with his captive in the process before getting shot.

Apparently, the remaining Colombians had somehow pieced together the Mexican cartel was involved, so even though Edward was technically dead and out of the business, he'd felt compelled to help his brother-in-law, whom he'd dragged into the operation. And they needed Jacob's assistance and connections. In terms of missions and Jacob's involvement—this was minor compared to past jobs.

He needed to calm Taren's concerns about saying the wrong thing—she was his number one priority. Changing the subject to her shopping seemed like a good way to do that.

"So, who are the magnets for?"

"Me. I always need magnets."

He remembered. Her fridge had been her bulletin board—anything she wanted to have a reminder or a safe place for was stuck on her refrigerator: coupons, upcoming concert tickets, appointment reminders.... All secured with magnets outside her Frigidaire.

The memory made him smile. He was glad she hadn't changed.

"What?" she said with an accusing tone when she noticed his smile.

He shook his head. "Nothing, baby. Absolutely nothing. My refrigerator is extra-large so you'll have all kinds of room for your magnets. We should probably buy more."

She slowed her gait. "I haven't agreed to move in with you. I still don't know if I'm taking the job in New Orleans yet."

He didn't want her taking the job—any job, but he did want her moving in with him. One obstacle at a time.

With his hand on her back, he urged her forward. "We've got a week to worry about that. And five more ports of call to get more magnets."

The idea of more shopping brought a smile to her face. He loved that something as simple as ceramic refrigerator tchotchkes made her happy. God, he hoped their kids got her temperament. The two of them were in for a rough eighteen plus years otherwise if they got his.

When he stopped and thought about it, he really had no idea what she saw in him. She obviously didn't love him for his money or power, he was broody as fuck, and distrusted—and disliked—pretty much everyone on the planet. Well, everyone except Taren and his parents, and he'd probably include his brother Jack, along with Edward and Reagan, and Bella and Dante in that equation, as well. Anyone else... no, not really. Meanwhile, Taren tried to see the good in everyone.

Unfortunately, there was little good in the people he associated with. It wasn't like they called him when they were at their best—just the opposite. He only entered the picture when their situation had gone completely sideways, and they'd be fucked without him. Which is why he was able to charge an exorbitant rate, and why they were willing to pay it. He was the best mercenary fixer money could buy.

Not that he didn't earn his money. He'd earned every red cent he made, and then some. But now... now he was thinking maybe he'd take his money at forty and slow down. Be a husband and a dad. Probably not retire completely, but definitely ease back, and his rates were going up substantially to help quell the demand for his services. Maybe he'd even take on a partner someday.

The thought actually felt liberating, so he knew it was the right decision. When she entwined her fingers with his and grinned up at him as they approached a man pushing a silver cart marked, *Helado*, he'd never been more sure. There was his future; standing next to him, holding his hand and waiting for an ice cream cone.

"I love you, Tink," he said as he squeezed her fingers with his.

She didn't say it back, just squeezed his fingers in return with a smile. He wasn't worried—he knew she loved him, deep down; she just needed a little time to come to terms with it. Jacob had kind of overwhelmed her the last three days. He was a patient man.

And she was worth the wait.

Chapter Eighteen

Taren

She'd had so much fun exploring the little shops and haggling with the vendors. She loved that Jacob was with her, always keeping a watchful eye on her but letting her do her thing. She felt safe while at the same time free. She'd never felt that way with David. He was always shaking his head in disapproval if she said the wrong thing or acted the wrong way. That was why she was a little worried about meeting Edward's wife and in-laws. She'd been known to make a social blunder or two.

"Should we get one for Edward and our driver?" she asked as they looked at the menu of frozen treats.

"Yes, to the driver. Fuck no about Edward. He can get his own."

She pursed her lips and shot him a disapproving look before ordering three vanilla cones.

"What do you want?" she asked, looking at Jacob.

"I haven't had an ice cream cone in seven years, Tink, I have no idea."

"Make that four," she said to the vendor, holding up four fingers.

She paid the man and handed Jake two of the cones the vendor offered, then took the other two.

Edward walked up to them and Jacob shoved the cone at him.

"Here," he snarled.

"Aw, thanks."

"Don't thank me, I said not to get you one."

Edward threw his arm around Taren's shoulder and took a bite of the ice cream.

"Thanks, that was really thoughtful."

"My pleasure," she said with a smile.

Edward kept his arm around her, and as they approached the car, she heard Jacob growl, "You can remove your arm now."

Taren felt Edward chuckle as he took his arm off her. She gave the surprised driver his ice cream, then stood outside the car, even though it was obvious Jacob and Edward were waiting for her to get in before they did.

"Finish your cones first, and let him"—she gestured to the driver—"finish his before he has to start driving."

Jacob put his arm around her and pulled her close to him, while Edward teased, "She's way too good for you, man."

"Yeah, I know."

"But he's amazing in bed," she said with a straight face as she took a bite of the cone.

The two men seemed stunned she'd said that, then started laughing.

"I like you even more now," Edward said before ducking into the backseat, out of Jacob's reach.

"That was funny," Jake said.

She shrugged and popped the last bit of cone into her mouth. "It's true. You are amazing."

He leaned down and murmured in her ear, "So are you," then smacked her ass as she got into the car.

****

Jacob

They pulled through the guard gates at Bella and Dante's estate, and on instinct, Jacob felt for the gun Edward had slipped him, just like Jacob had requested before agreeing to be in attendance today. Sometimes he really hated jackets—especially in the summer heat, but it was a casualty of packing a weapon. It was either that or tuck it in his waistband and leave his shirt untucked, which he wasn't going to do for a business meeting.

Jacob wasn't sure why he was so on edge. He'd been to the Guzmans' several times, worked with Mrs. Guzman when she was known as Kennedy Jones in the agency, and knew her husband vouched for all the men coming today. He deduced his uneasiness was due to Taren being there.

The second they walked through the door, Edward's wife, Reagan—who was also Bella's sister, embraced him in a hug.

"It's so good to see you again."

"Babe, this is Jacob's girlfriend, Taren," Edward offered gleefully.

Reagan threw her arms around Taren like she was a long lost sister.

"I'm so happy to meet you! We love Jacob so much; we'll be forever indebted to him for all his help in…"

"Reagan," Jacob interrupted sternly. She looked over at him, and he cocked an eyebrow at her in warning.

"Oh, sorry," she said rolling her eyes. "I always forget the first rule of Fight Club."

"Ha. Ha. Where's this beautiful baby girl of yours? What did you name her?" he asked, changing the subject.

"Brianna Kennedy—and she just went down for a nap. But I expect Madi will be venturing in with the nanny at any minute."

He hadn't seen Bella and Dante's daughter since she was probably just a few months old; the little girl had to be two or three by now.

"Speak of the devil," Edward said as his niece came running through the French doors leading to the pool and the immaculate grounds surrounding it.

Mr. and Mrs. Guzman appeared from the hallway across the room, and Dante scooped up his daughter as she streaked by him just as a young woman in her late twenties, with her hair falling out of her ponytail, rushed through the doorway looking frantic. Jacob noticed her knee was bleeding.

"We've got her, Carmen. Go have lunch," the Mexican man said to the younger woman.

"I'm sorry. She's just so quick, and I tripped chasing after her."

"Oh, no!" Bella quickly responded. "Are you okay?"

"It's just a scrape," Carmen replied. "I'll go get it cleaned up."

"We've got my sister here to help, why don't you take the rest of the day off?" Bella suggested and was met with a look of panic until she added, "It will be paid, of course, since we scheduled you for the entire day."

"Okay, if you're sure you don't need me," the young woman reluctantly agreed, her eyes darting between Dante holding his daughter and Bella standing next to him. She didn't turn to leave until Dante nodded his head and said, "We're sure."

They were a beautiful family; Bella with her stunning red hair and porcelain skin, Dante a classic and distinguished Mexican Mafioso, and their daughter a hybrid of the two, having her mother's green eyes and button nose, but her father's coloring and high cheekbones.

Bella turned toward the visitors and warmly greeted them.

"Jacob, so nice to see you."

He wasn't sure how he was going to be received, since Bella had at one point told him if she ever saw him again, she'd kill him.

"You look well, Bella. I like the hair."

When she first left the agency, she had been dying it brown when she had been trying to stay hidden while everyone thought she was dead. Well everyone but Edward and another agent.

"Dante's contacts have assured him the CIA has me listed as deceased, so I've been feeling a little braver."

"That's the word on the street, too," Jacob offered in reassurance. "I've not heard otherwise; for either you or Edward. I'll let you know if that changes."

"We appreciate that, Jacob," Dante said, while his daughter Madison, stared at Jacob intently.

Bella also noticed her daughter's fascination with him and said, "Madi, can you say hello to Mr. Jacob?"

"Hello, Mr. Jacob," a tiny voice echoed, as her father set her on her feet.

"Hi, Madi. This is my friend, Taren," he said, putting his hand on Tinkerbell's arm.

The little girl was not impressed with Jacob's girlfriend and didn't offer a greeting until her mother prompted her to, then she obliged in the same sweet voice, "Hi, Taren."

She hadn't stopped staring at Jacob, so he bent down on one knee, and she immediately came to him. Her parents exchanged bewildered looks, as Dante murmured, "She doesn't go to anyone but me and Bella. Not even her nanny."

"Jacob, do you want to see my new dollhouse?" Madison asked, slipping her little toddler hand into his great big one.

He glanced up at the adults with their varying looks of astonishment and couldn't help but grin at them.

"Sure. Can Taren come too?"

"No, thank you, that's okay," Madison replied politely, making everyone except her mother giggle.

"Madison," Bella said in warning. "Miss Taren can see your dollhouse, too."

"Well, I want to see this dollhouse," Edward said.

"Me, too," Reagan chimed in.

"Go show them your dollhouse, baby," Dante encouraged.

With her hand still in Jacob's, she led the way to her bedroom, ignoring everyone but Jacob once they got out of earshot of her parents. As godmother, Reagan took on the responsibility of making sure the little girl answered when anyone but Jacob asked her questions.

"Wow, your bedroom is like a princess's," Taren said, as she looked up at the high ceilings and bright natural light when they walked in the pink room that was bigger than his first house.

"Are you a princess?" he asked Madison.

"Mmm hmm," she confidently agreed like only a three-year-old could. He couldn't help but smile at her self-assurance. He hoped his daughters would have moxie like hers. "Here's my dollhouse, Jacob."

He responded with the appropriate awe and wonder. He wasn't that familiar with dollhouses, having only one younger brother, but this one seemed to put any that he'd seen to shame. Definitely cartel princess worthy. Although, to be fair, Dante was trying to go legit with his pot dispensaries throughout the United States, and seemed to be making a nice profit with his new venture.

"Let's play, Jacob." Madison said, handing him a male doll then began fishing through a box full of dolls until she pulled out a dark haired one. "You be the papa, and I'll be the mama."

He looked over at the other three grownups, all grinning from their seats at a miniature table and chairs that was set up for a tea party. Taren shot him a wink while Edward raised his plastic tea cup in a toast.

Madison hopped her doll towards his in the dollhouse, and in her tiny voice, asked, "*Hola, mi amor.* How was your day?"

He looked directly at Taren and winked back as he moved his doll in response. "Perfect, darlin'. I came home to you."

Chapter Nineteen

Taren

Her ovaries couldn't take much more of this. When Bella and Dante's daughter moved and sat on Jacob's lap while they played dolls, it was all she could do not to tackle him right there in front of everyone.

Bella appeared at the doorway holding her niece, who was fussing.

"Look who woke up," the beautiful redhead said as she bounced the baby in her arms, trying to soothe her.

Edward started to rise from the small table where the three had been chatting, but Reagan put her hand on his arm.

"She's probably hungry. I'll go feed her."

After handing the baby off, Bella looked at her daughter sitting on Jacob's lap and offering explicit instructions on how their make believe was to go, and smiled like she'd witnessed this exchange before. Taren imagined Dante was probably a hands-on dad, and had played dolls with his daughter plenty of times. She had an amazing vocabulary for a three-year-old; something that was usually acquired from receiving a lot of attention.

"Lunch is ready, everyone."

Madison stood and reached for Jacob's hand. "Come on, Jacob. You can sit by me."

"Let's wait for Taren," he said gently as he held his other hand out toward her.

With a smile, Taren took his hand, and the three headed back downstairs with Edward and Bella following behind.

She heard Edward say to Bella, "John might have been replaced. I think your daughter has a crush on Jacob."

Watching the handsome man as he engaged in a spirited conversation about unicorns with the toddler, Taren thought, *Who could blame her?* She was crushing on him pretty hard at the moment, too.

They were escorted into an elaborate dining room with chandeliers and the longest table she'd ever seen. It was made of dark wood and had ornate legs with claw feet every sixth seat. She performed a quick count and determined it was designed to hold seventy-four people; thirty-six on each side, plus one at each end. Right now, it was set for seven, plus a high chair, on the end of the room where they first came through the door, and she wondered who else would be joining them.

Her question was answered when Dante walked in with a man with jet black hair, blue eyes, and cheekbones that rivaled Jacob's.

Wow. She looked at the people around the table being directed to their seat assignments by the precocious three-year-old. It was like Taren was having lunch at a model convention. She was definitely out of her league.

Jake squeezed her fingers and gave her a quick wink before releasing her hand to pull out her chair for her, and she felt a big smile spread across her face, unable to stop it. She loved how important he made her feel.

"No, Papa," the little girl suddenly yelled. "Uncle Jacob is sitting there!"

"*Uncle* Jacob?" Edward, who really was her uncle, said with one eyebrow raised, clearly offended at having to share the title.

"Hey, don't look at me," Jacob said, still standing.

"Uncle Jacob is going to sit there," Dante corrected her, pointing to the chair across from Bella and to his immediate right from the head of the table. The high chair was situated on the corner to his left, between Madison's parents.

"No!" she wailed, throwing her sippy cup to the ground.

"Madison Belle Guzman," Dante said with authority, lowering his voice rather than raising it. It was evident he meant business, even to Taren.

Apparently the little girl realized it, too, because she quickly ceased her temper tantrum and looked down as if ashamed.

Dante quietly reached over and caressed his daughter's downy hair in approval.

"*Esto es mejor mijita princesa,*" he murmured.

That's better, my little princess.

Taren's Spanish wasn't that great, but she understood that. She wasn't sure who Dante Guzman was, but there was no doubt the man wielded power. Everyone in the room seemed to recognize it, even his daughter—who appeared to have him wrapped around her little finger.

"John, how have you been?" Jacob asked the gorgeous dark haired man who was seated next to Bella.

"Uncle John!" Madison's small voice rang out, seeming to just realize the other man was there, even though she'd just directed him where to sit two minutes ago.

While the other man talked with Jacob and acknowledged the toddler, Taren leaned to her side and quietly teased Edward, "How come it doesn't bother you when she calls him *uncle*?"

He replied with a smirk. "He's her godfather. He outranks me."

"Ahhh." She smiled and sat up straight.

She felt Jacob's hand on her knee, and he softly squeezed it when she brought her hand on top of his.

Reagan appeared with a chubby, bald baby who seemed content to sit on her mother's lap while her father beamed at his progeny from across the table.

Two older Mexican women in grey uniforms pushed a cart through the door and began to serve lunch. It smelled amazing as the plate was set in front of her. Taren observed everyone murmuring their thanks and addressing the women by name. But it wasn't until Dante boomed, "Rosa, Maria, as usual, you've outdone yourselves. *Gracias*," did the women smile like they were appreciated.

They then fussed over Madison, making sure she was going to eat the gourmet toddler lunch they'd prepared for her.

"*Es muy rico*," Bella assured them in Spanish, while Dante prompted, "Tell Abuela Maria and Abuela Rosa thank you."

"*Gracias abuelas!*" The little girl parroted her father.

"I love how bilingual she is," Taren said quietly to Jacob.

"Our kids are going to be that way, too" he promised with another squeeze to her knee before removing his hand to eat lunch.

As she listened to the banter among the group, she couldn't help but think how ordinary it all seemed. Ordinary except for the maids serving them at a table so long, she'd only seen something like it in the movies, and them being at an estate with armed guards at the gates and along the perimeter.

Maybe that's what she was having a hard time reconciling—the people she was having lunch with seemed like people she'd meet every day, yet the circumstances didn't match. Would Madison even understand someday when she was older that most people didn't live in mansions, with cooks and maids? That it was unusual to have a driver take her everywhere or have armed guards at her home?

Is that how Taren's life was going to be from now on? Would she try to normalize the abnormal for their children?

A sense of panic rose up through her, and Jake's arm came around her shoulders as he whispered in her ear, "I feel your wheels turning, Tink. Time to apply the brakes, baby."

Taren looked up at him helplessly, and he hugged her shoulder in return.

"It's going to be okay. I promise. Just breathe."

She nodded and took a deep breath, feeling the warmth of his arm touching her shoulders. It was funny, but with his assurances—both with his words and his body, she *did* feel better. How was it possible that he had such an effect on her?

He looked at her and smiled, then resumed eating his lunch, but kept his arm around the back of her chair.

****

Jacob

After lunch, Edward suggested his wife and Taren take the children to the nursery before the others arrived. Jacob realized the former agent was concerned about his wife and child as much as he was about Taren, and he appreciated that. Bella disappeared with them, effectively answering his unspoken question about whether she'd be in attendance at the meeting.

Jacob hadn't done a lot of work with the cartel, but he'd done enough to know the drill.

Today's players were from other syndicates who had ties to the Guzman family and were being affected by the

Colombians, as well as Dante's uncle, Ramon—the head of the family. There were going to be some heavy hitters in the room, all vying to be the top dog. The machismo was going to be flowing steadily this afternoon; Jacob would show them all respect and sit back, answering their questions, but only offering advice when asked. He didn't need to swing his dick around to know he was really the one running this whole thing. They all knew it, too.

Ramon was the first to arrive and remarked to Jacob when he walked through the door of Dante's office, "I see you brought a friend to Ensenada."

Jacob knew some of Dante's men were on Ramon's payroll, and Ramon liked to think he still had his finger on the pulse of Ensenada, even though he was living large in San Diego, so Jacob wasn't surprised with Ramon's comment— even though that was clearly the patrón's intent.

Casually picking up his glass of Scotch from the side table next to where he was seated in a burgundy leather wingback chair, Jacob took a drink before replying, "Surely you understand having needs that only a woman can fulfill, Ramon?" The mercenary raised his eyebrow. "Or is there another reason you're still single?"

Jacob knew questioning the man's sexuality would get his hackles up, and hopefully, take the focus off Taren.

"Ask the women still recovering in my bed from last night," Ramon spat back, causing Jacob to chuckle to himself. Sometimes people were just too easy to predict.

Miguel Hernandez, the self-proclaimed, *El Rey*—the king arrived next, followed closely behind by the other invited men. John quietly slipped in from a side door and sat down next to Jacob, while Edward stood in the back of the room. Bella's presence was missed, but her absence was probably for the best. A woman at this meeting would have stood out and there would have been unwanted questions. She was trying to fly as far under the radar as possible— hiding in plain sight from both the CIA and the cartel, since she'd killed the previous Guzman patrón, El Jefe Enrique Guzman, when she was still an agency operative. She seemed content with consulting behind the scenes and raising her daughter these days.

Dante's deep voice boomed out, getting everyone's attention, and discussion about the next steps started.

"And what if they don't agree to this truce?" *El Rey* asked.

"They will," Jacob replied confidently.

"How can you be so sure?"

"Because their operation has been crippled. The CIA has picked up their investigation of the human trafficking again after the women the Colombians were holding captive to sell were brought to the US and testified."

"So why did they start this damn war to begin with?" Ramon snarled.

Jacob shrugged. "Pride. Self-preservation. To discourage it from happening again. They needed to show they wouldn't take such a thing without retaliating."

"You did this to all of us, Dante," Francisco Gomez snapped, which was a mistake, because Ramon took the reprimand of his nephew personally, and the pissing contest began.

John seemed as content as Jacob to sit back and watch the scene unfold, while Edward slipped out the door before the focus turned to him—since he was really the one who got everyone into this mess.

Dante, for his part, never threw Edward under the bus, instead citing his reason for being in Colombia as exploring expansion opportunities when he got tangled up in a CIA operation. He reported he had thought the Colombians double-crossed him.

All of it was a lie, of course. Dante had flown his wife down on his private jet so she could assist in the rescue of Edward's brother, Marcus with the help of Edward and some CIA agents from Marcus' team. All in order to get her sister back, who Edward had kidnapped as 'incentive' for Bella to help him. They probably would have gotten away unknown had Edward not been shot and rushed to the hospital. Jacob had paid a handsome amount—in US dollars—for 'no questions asked', and that allowed Edward surgery and treatment enough to stabilize him so they could get him the hell out of the country—on Dante's private jet. It had taken some time, but according to Jacob's sources, the Colombians eventually traced Edward leaving the hospital and getting on Dante's jet to the events that took place. And the retaliation against the Sinaloa cartel began.

"Gentlemen, can we get back to the task at hand?" Jacob asked loudly, trying to rein in the chaos that had ensued in Dante's study.

"So when is this meeting with the intermediary taking place?" Miguel asked after the noise had died down.

"It's set for the day after tomorrow in Miami."

"I want you there," Ramon declared, directing his attention to Jacob.

He shook his head. "I'm afraid I'm not available."

"Become available. Whatever it costs, I don't care. We want you there representing us."

"It's not about the money."

"What's the problem then?"

When Jacob refused to elaborate, a look of recognition flashed in Ramon's eyes and a small smile formed on the man's lips.

Goddammit. Taren just became leverage—exactly what he'd been wanting to avoid.

"I'm sure you could change the location from Miami to wherever your port of call on Thursday is. It'd only be a minor disruption to your honeymoon. Surely your wife will understand," the patrón said smugly as he sought for confirmation to his fishing expedition based on Jacob's reaction.

Fucking assholes. Jacob schooled his features to hide how pissed he was. *This is going to cost the cartel.*

"I can be in Miami on Thursday on your behalf, but my fee is one million dollars—upfront. For the meeting alone. Any follow-up is extra."

Ramon didn't bat an eye. "Done. Let's talk about what we expect with this truce..."

He should have asked for more money.

Chapter Twenty

Jacob

"Then I'm getting off the ship, too," Taren declared when he told her he was only boarding to get some of his things.

"No, Tink. I'll meet up with you in Acapulco on Friday," Jacob assured her.

Her pout said it all.

He pinched the bridge of his nose; the Guzmans were going to be pissed, but she trumped everyone. Picking up his secure phone and stepping onto the balcony, he called Scotty, his pilot, first. He'd planned on driving to San Diego and flying commercial out of San Diego International on Wednesday night, but, glancing at Taren through the glass door, he decided that idea wasn't going to work.

"I need you to arrive in Puerto Vallarta Wednesday night for an early departure on Thursday morning then returning to Acapulco later that day."

At least this way he'd only be away from her for one day and one night.

After confirming with Scotty, he called Edward to let him know not to expect his return to the estate.

"Dante isn't going to like this," the younger man warned.

"Tell him not to worry about it. I'll be in Miami in time for the meeting. He can email me any concerns he has."

Jacob disconnected the call and shut his phone off. He needed some Tinkerbell time. He'd been staring at her all day and unable to put his hands on her properly, like he'd wanted.

"I'm set to leave out of Puerto Vallarta Thursday morning," he told her when he walked back inside and sat down next to her on the couch, where she'd curled up with her Kindle.

She looked at him with a wide smile, set the reading device down, and scurried to sit up on her knees.

"You mean you're staying on board?" she said with wide eyes and an excited smile.

He leaned toward her; feeling like a wolf ready to pounce on its prey. She was so damn adorable, and he was wrapped around her finger—which made him want to fuck her even more. Not because he resented it; on the contrary, because he relished it.

"I'm staying on board until Thursday, but getting off first thing. I'll meet you in in Acapulco when the ship arrives on Friday morning."

"Can I go with you?"

"No."

He didn't offer an explanation where he was going or why; she was a smart girl though. He knew she'd figure out it was the result of today's meeting, and hopefully not ask anything further.

"No?" She began to caress his cock over his slacks. "Please?"

Her tactic wasn't going to work, but he appreciated the effort.

Jacob grabbed her wrists, brought her hands to her sides, and reiterated, "No," then tugged the top of her sundress below her tits and began to fondle her round globes over the material of her bra, dipping his thumbs under the fabric and grazing her nipples as he watched her face.

"I was really proud of you today," he said, his voice husky with need. "You were charming without offering too many details. Yet, they all felt like they got to know you by the time we left, and they loved you."

He pulled her bra down so her boobs were bared to him; her nipples stiff and ready to be sucked.

"Not as much as I love you, though," Jacob murmured as he dipped his mouth to a rosy peak, swirling his tongue around the pebbled flesh before sucking it between his teeth. Her body began to wobble and her hands came around the back of his head, as if to steady herself.

"Oh, god, Jake. That feels so good," she moaned as she widened her knees in invitation.

Jacob couldn't help but smile around her nipple. He loved how responsive she was to his touch.

He switched tits, suckling her right while pinching and squeezing her left; pushing her onto her back on the couch in the process. He reached under her skirt and slid her panties to the side, plunging a finger into her wet cunt as he continued devouring her boobs with his mouth.

Her gasps spurred him on, and he spread her juices to her clit, circling it with his thumb while he moved his ring finger in and out of her. She began to move in rhythm against his hand and he slipped a second finger inside her, causing her to inhale sharply, then let out a long moan.

"Oh, yessss," she hissed, tilting her hips forward.

"You like that, baby?" he growled with his teeth around her nipple.

"Mmm hmm," she whimpered in a high pitch.

"Are you going to come for me?"

"Ohhhhh," was her long response as she dropped her legs farther open and cupped her tit to push it back in his mouth, holding a fistful of his hair in her other hand when she did.

His cock was leaking. Her wantonness was so damn sexy.

Jacob began fingering her faster, increasing the pressure and tempo on her clit with his thumb while he voraciously sucked her tits. Jacob could feel her pussy getting wetter as her body began to clench, and he knew she was right on the edge of orgasm.

He bit down on her nipple, harder than he had earlier when he teased her boobs, and just as he did, she began to thrash and buck under him, chanting, "Oh, god," like she was praying.

Making her come brought him immense satisfaction; a small part of him had the urge to beat his chest like a caveman, but an even bigger part wanted his cock inside her—*now*.

While she lie on the couch, trembling in her post orgasmic state, he toed off his shoes and socks, and dropped his slacks and underwear to the floor then pulled hers off too, before pushing his cock inside her without a word.

He bit back a groan.

Goddamn, did she feel good.

Really good.

So good he was afraid to move for fear of lasting all of thirty-six more seconds.

He thought of every baseball and football statistic he could as he slowly began thrusting in and out of her.

I wonder if that longer lasting spray I've seen advertised really works?

"Fuuuuck," he growled, burying his face in her neck. He loved how her neck smelled when she was just a little sweaty. It was one of his favorite scents.

Her skin is so damn soft.

I wish I could fuck her forever.

Unfortunately, that wasn't going to be the case tonight.

He started thrusting with a steady pace, then she lifted her legs, changing the angle ever-so-slightly and caused him to lose control.

Jacob didn't fight it, instead began to fuck her rapidly as he felt his balls tighten, then held her hips tight and roared when he began to spurt rope after rope of cum inside her walls.

She was smiling seductively up at him when he finally opened his eyes.

"Damn, you're beautiful," he panted, trying to catch his breath and slow his heart rate before pulling out. He dropped down on his elbows and enveloped her body with his. She fit perfectly against him, and he knew she was the missing piece in his life.

"I love you, Tink," he whispered against her hair, then lifted his head to look into her eyes.

"I love you, too," she uttered softly then kissed his neck.

He closed his eyes and smiled, offering up a prayer of thanks to the powers that be for this perfect moment.

****

Taren

She knew she loved Jake and would be miserable without him, but continued trying to reconcile how different her life was going to be with him in it.

Today had been an interesting example.

"So, am I going to be able to have friends if I move to New Orleans? Will we have parties and invite other couples over?" she asked with her head on his chest as they lie in bed before going down to a late dinner.

"Of course you'll have friends. Everyone loves you, Tink. Unfortunately, you're going to be married to a salty old bastard who tolerates people, at best. But I promise if you want to have a party, or other couples over, I will show up and behave myself—after properly vetting everyone, of course. I'll even make small talk. I *know* how to be social, I just don't *like* being social, unless I'm with you."

"You'll have to vet our friends?"

"Yeah, baby. I will. That's part of my world."

"What will we say you do for a living?"

She felt him shrug. "Same thing I've always said. I'm a security consultant."

Taren lifted her head and looked at him sharply.

"You never said you were a *security* consultant."

"Yes, I did."

"No, you didn't," Taren insisted. "I would have remembered that."

"So what kind of consultant did you think I was?"

Looking back, she realized how naïve she had really been. *Dumb and in love.*

She laid her head back down on him, slightly embarrassed.

"I don't know. I thought like marketing or something."

His chuckle rumbled in her ear through his chest. "Why would you have thought that?"

"I honestly have no idea, other than the only consultant I've ever known was when I worked in retail in high school, and the store hired a marketing specialist and our sales doubled. I figured you were like that—going in and saving the day."

"You're not wrong. Most of the time, that's exactly what I do—save the day. Which is why I get paid so much money. I'm making a million dollars when I'm gone on Thursday."

She practically choked on air when she picked her head back up.

"A *million* dollars? Are you serious? Is that normal?"

"In the past, no. My rate wasn't that high, but it's going to be from here on out. I really don't want to work as much as I used to."

She couldn't help but smile when she sat up and straddled him.

"You don't? Why not? What do you want to do?" she teased.

He positioned her hips over his cock.

"I want to spend my time naked with you."

She began to rock gently on his hardening dick.

"I don't know... I might develop an expensive shopping habit knowing you're making a million dollars a day."

"First of all, it's not a million dollars a day, every day. But regardless, you can shop all you want, baby. I've got plenty of money for you to buy whatever your little heart desires."

"How about a normal life?"

"Normal is relative, Tink."

With a sigh of, "I know," she collapsed back onto his chest where his arms promptly came around her.

"We're going to have great adventures, baby."

"No, *you're* going to have great adventures while I wait at home for you to finish then come back."

"Stop pouting about Thursday. I'll be back Friday, and we'll enjoy the rest of the cruise together."

"You're right. I just hate not knowing where you're going or why."

He didn't take the bait and cave, much to her chagrin. Instead, he held firm, telling her, "I'm sorry. It's better for everyone that you don't know."

The truth was, she *did* know he was going to Miami. She just wanted him to be the one to tell her instead of overhearing it. She still didn't know why and wasn't exactly sure she wanted to know. It was more the idea that he'd be willing to tell her if she wanted him to.

"If you're hungry, you better get up. Otherwise, I'm going to fuck you again."

She sat up straight, her hips still straddling his.

"You're so crass," she teasingly admonished, all the while moving her center gently over his cock.

He playfully swatted her ass. "Last chance for food," he warned as he gripped her hips.

Now that she thought about it, she *was* hungry...

"Okay, okay! I'm going to get ready!" she giggled as she scampered off him and headed toward her cabin.

"Wear the green dress!" he called after her.

She poked her head back around the corner. "We'll see."

He raised his eyebrows. "Guess what's going to happen if you don't?"

Taren couldn't help but smile as she stood in front of her armoire, deciding whether or not she was going to be a brat and wear the red and navy dress. She eventually pulled the green one from its hanger, reasoning there'd be plenty of other ways she could be put over his knee if she changed her mind.

Chapter Twenty-One

Jacob

He was the first one off the ship Thursday morning, with a driver waiting to take him to the airport where his plane was ready to fly him the four hours to Miami. If there wasn't the three-hour time difference, he'd be getting there in plenty of time; but with not being able to disembark the ship until 7:00 a.m., he was going to be cutting it close.

It'd been harder than he thought to leave Tink sleeping in bed. After staring at her delicate features for a long time, it was all he could to keep from scooping her up in his arms and holding her. But, he didn't want to be selfish and wake her, so he left her asleep with a rose and sappy as fuck love note on his pillow.

She'd turned his world upside down again, just like she had when he first met her. And he loved it.

Jacob boarded the plane, and they were in the air moments later. He was on a video conference call with Dante, Ramon, John, and Edward almost the entire flight, more to offer reassurances than to strategize. He'd had a plan developed before he'd even left Dante's on Tuesday.

"I still wish you would have been here Tuesday night to go over things again," Dante grumbled after everyone else had disconnected.

"We're going over them now," Jacob replied, unfazed at Dante's displeasure.

"Bella seems to really like your girl."

"Me, too."

"Well, when you retire from the mercenary profession, I'm always in need of help with the dispensary business."

"Thanks, I'll keep that in mind. Although, I'd probably be more apt to become your competition."

"Why do you think I'm making the offer? Maybe we could look at a partnership."

"I think you'd better clear that with your other partners first."

"Bella, John, and I already talked about it after you left the other night. Bella was the one who brought it up, actually. She said she wouldn't be surprised if this was your last mission."

She wasn't far off. The more time he spent with Taren, the more he thought about retiring—but it was going to be hard to do, especially without a partner.

"I'm keeping my options open," Jacob replied noncommittally.

"Well, keep us in mind."

"Will do."

Scotty's voice came from overhead, telling him they were about to start their descent into Miami.

Dante must have heard him, because he said, "I'll talk to you later. Let me know how it goes today."

"I'll call you when I'm back on the jet," Jacob responded before hanging up.

He wasn't especially worried about the meeting. Jacob had already been talking with the Colombians' go-between, so he knew they didn't want to be at war with the Sinaloans; they couldn't afford it. They'd retaliated to save face over Dante being involved when their human trafficking victims were freed, along with the CIA agent they had been holding for ransom. Now, they were getting a sit-down truce negotiation; another pride-saving gesture.

The reality was if Ramon wanted to, he could wipe out the Cartagenans in less than a month. But Ramon wasn't interested in exerting the time, manpower, or money it would take, so he was willing to negotiate an end to the little skirmish before it became an outright war. Ramon had bigger fish to fry—Los Zetas had been encroaching on his territory to the west, and he was gearing up for that fight.

Jacob anticipated today was going to be nothing more than formalities.

Three hours later, he was on the plane back to Mexico with an agreed upon truce with terms even better than Ramon had wanted. He was going to just miss the ship leaving port in Puerto Vallarta, so he had Scotty take him into Acapulco, where he'd board first thing in the morning, have breakfast with Tink, then spend the day sightseeing and shopping in the city with her, watching her joy at negotiating for two dollar trinkets. That idea made him infinitely happier than the multi-million dollar deal he just brokered.

Taren

She woke up by herself, feeling lonely until she read Jacob's love letter, softly tracing the rose he'd left over her face and lips as she did.

Tinkerbell,

When you threw your arms around me on the lido deck on Sunday afternoon, it felt like my dead heart started beating again. It died seven long years ago; that day on your doorstep when I made the biggest mistake of my life and broke both our hearts. I know it will take time to earn your trust again, but I'm prepared to wait as long as you need to believe in me once more.

I have no other choice, Tink. I need you like I need air.

I promise I'll be back first thing tomorrow morning, and I'll try to text you later this afternoon on the phone I gave you.

Until then, know you're always in my thoughts.

I love you.

J.

She reread the letter at least fifty times before breakfast and didn't even get off the ship in Puerto Vallarta, instead spent the day poolside finishing Misty Malloy's trilogy, in between rereading the letter, dozing in the sun, and having lunch. Oh, and meeting a crazy bachelorette party that she was going to dinner with.

She went back to her cabin before dinner and checked the phone Jacob had given her in Ensenada. Her heart skipped a beat when she saw the notification bar alerting her to a waiting message.

Unfortunately, going to just miss getting on board before you leave Puerto Vallarta.

She returned an emoji with a face crying tears.

I know, baby. I feel the same way. I'll be waiting at the gangway when the ship arrives in the morning. We'll have breakfast on board?

Smiling, she typed her response. *I'd like that.*

How was your day today? Did you like Puerto Vallarta?

I didn't go on shore.

Why not?

Giving his question some thought, she finally responded. *I don't know. I was nervous to go without you.*

That might be for the best, baby. I like that you're thinking about your safety. So what did you do today?

I miss you. Was today successful?

I miss you, too. Today was good. Why aren't you answering me about what you did today?

Unable to keep a straight face, she smiled as her fingers flew over the keypad. *I wish you were here.*

She was purposefully being a brat, knowing that it would drive him crazy not being here to do anything about it.

Tinkerbell, were you naughty today? Is that why you're not answering me?

Her smile growing, she answered that question. *No, I laid by the pool and read.*

Were you alone the whole time?

Well, no.

She wasn't technically. The wait staff who kept her hydrated, and the loud bachelorette party next to her at the pool who adopted her into their group, kept her company all day. But it was fun being vague and making him think there was more to the story.

Maybe it would make him think twice about leaving her next time.

What do you mean no?

Was he scowling when he typed that question? Perhaps his hand was twitching? With a final flurry of her fingers, she sent her last text. *My dinner companions are here; I'll text you later when I get back from dinner.*

She shut the phone off before he replied, and threw it back in her colorful bag like it was hot: in part because she was afraid to see his response, but also to keep from caving and telling him the truth too soon. He needed to stew on it for a little while before she came clean, which she was planning on doing as soon as she got back from dinner with the bachelorettes.

She had a feeling her ass was going to be red tomorrow once he got back on board. The thought made her clench her thighs together in anticipation.

****

Jacob

She thought she was so clever. She must have forgotten when he'd told her that he'd planted cameras not only in his room for security, but also throughout her room. He saw the group of rowdy women arrive at her door and come inside the suite as she finished getting ready.

They looked like they were having fun—one girl had a sash across her body and a crown on her head, so he assumed this was a bachelorette party that Tink had probably started talking to, and they realized she was alone and absorbed her into their group. Two of the girls were carrying champagne bottles and passing them around like they were a group of winos sharing hooch. He was happy to see Taren shake her head when the bottle was offered to her.

His girl was too cute for words in her lavender sundress with matching cardigan, white sandals, and her hair pulled back in a wide dark purple headband. She looked like a kindergarten teacher or PTA president—vastly different from the other women in her group who were in sequined mini-dresses and four inch heels.

"I feel like I should change," he heard her say to a tall brunette who had carried in a bottle.

"Why? You look cute—very preppy."

"Well, yeah, but I'm not exactly matching what you guys are wearing."

The brunette cocked her head. "Didn't you say you have a boyfriend? Honey, we're all trying to get laid—except for the bride of course, but this is kind of her last hurrah, so I think she's hoping to at least get felt up."

Jacob felt his grip tighten on the phone where he was watching the events taking place. Nobody better feel his Tinkerbell up. Visions of Peter and Jeff trying flashed into his mind.

Fuck, this was going to be a long night.

****

Just two hours later, his phone alerted there was movement in her cabin, and Jacob picked up to watch her come in alone and change out of her clothes into a baby pink pajama set, then fish through her bag and pull out the burner phone he'd given her.

She shut the lights off in her room, but instead of going to bed, the motion sensors in his room went off and his bedside lamp switched on. With a knowing smile, he waited for her to go through his things. He felt his chest tighten when instead of snooping through his belongings, she simply pulled one of his dirty shirts out of his suitcase and put it on, then got under the covers in his bed and held his pillow tight against her. She lay like that for a few moments before rolling onto her back and turning on the phone.

He could tell when she was reading his last text message to her, because her fingertips went to her lips as a small smile crept across her face. It turned him on how much she loved submitting to him. The newly added spanking dynamic was a definite bonus—one she seemed to enjoy as much as he did.

His other phone pinged with an incoming message from her. He couldn't help but smile reading her text.

I'm sorry. I know I've got a punishment coming for being a brat. Just so you know, I went to dinner with ladies I met at the pool. Not a single male joined us, and I came back to my cabin while they headed to the nightclub. You're the only man for me—you know that.

He didn't respond right away, contemplating his best course of action, when another text came in.

I miss you so much. I'm sleeping in your shirt because it smells like you. I'm sorry I teased you. I loved your letter.

I miss you, too, baby. I'll see you before you know it. Get some sleep—you're going to need your energy tomorrow. You're right; you've got a punishment coming.

He added one of those winking emojis for emphasis then watched her smile broadly as she read it.

Jacob was going to try to get some work done tonight, but knew it was going to be hard. The temptation to watch her all night was great. She stacked the pillows behind her back and began reading her Kindle, so fortunately, every time he checked on her, not much had changed until she dozed off.

The next time he looked at the video feed, she'd shut the lights off. Jacob decided he was drawing the line at turning on the night vision, instead choosing to get a few hours of shuteye, too. He found himself wishing he had her pillow to hug as he tried to sleep.

Chapter Twenty-Two

Taren

At first she thought she was dreaming when she woke up to the dawn's light coming through the cabin windows and found Jake's arms around her, her body wrapped in the warmth of his naked chest.

He must have noticed she was awake because he murmured, "Sorry to wake you, baby. It's still early, go back to sleep."

"How are you here?" she whispered and rolled over to examine his body, like she may still be dreaming.

"It helps that I have a lot of money, and I'm very good at bribing people."

"I don't understand..."

"I was notified when the ship docked at three thirty this morning, and paid the workers in charge of bringing the ship to port a hefty sum, along with a sob story about missing the boat yesterday. They checked my boarding documents, took my 'tip,' and let me on."

"It's probably just because you're handsome," she murmured and rolled back over into a spooning position. "I'm so happy you're here."

She finally felt like she could relax now that he was back and fell into a deep slumber until he roused her later that morning.

"Tinkerbell, wake up," he cooed softly. "We're going to miss breakfast."

"I don't care," she moaned into her pillow with her eyes still closed.

Taren felt his hands caress her butt and in between her thighs, causing her to widen her legs for him.

"You're going to need your strength, baby girl. You've got a punishment coming." His tone was teasing, but she knew he wasn't joking when he squeezed her bum hard. Her eyes flew open at the realization of what was in store for her today.

"Now?"

"No," he answered with a disingenuous smile. "I think I'll let you anticipate it over breakfast. Maybe even lunch. Go get ready."

"You're mean," she pouted on her way to the bathroom, but was secretly excited with this little game they were playing.

As she lathered her body in the shower stall, she closed her eyes and imagined it was Jake's hands touching her. It was like he had ESP, because she heard the bathroom door open and close, and seconds later he was stepping through the curtain, his hard cock jutting out from his body.

Damn, did she like his cock.

"Well, hello," she said, reaching out to stroke his length with her soapy hands.

Jake leaned down under the water and kissed her. She could taste toothpaste as his tongue began exploring her mouth while his hands traveled from her waist to her breasts, pushing the mounds of flesh higher then tugging on her nipples and gently twisting them between his fingers.

"You were a naughty girl last night, trying to make me jealous."

"I thought you said you were territorial," she teased and was met with him pinching her rosy peaks harder in response.

"You're pretty sassy for someone who has a spanking coming later," he admonished, pressing her against the shower wall while grinding his cock between her legs.

"Maybe I'm looking forward to it."

He shook his head, grinning at her. "You're not supposed to look forward to your spankings, my little fairy. I might have to find some other way to punish you."

"Li—like how?" she gulped.

The spankings and the power exchange had been erotic, as had his objectification of her. But pain wasn't really her kink, and she didn't think she'd enjoy anything more than being spanked with his hand.

Jacob moved his body so the warm water was raining down on her, then reached between her legs and began to move his fingers over her clit. She closed her eyes and let her head fall back against the white acrylic wall.

"I was thinking orgasm denial."

Her eyes opened in a flash.

"I don't think I would like that very much."

He smirked as he dipped his fingers inside her then smeared her juices to her clit.

"You might be surprised. Besides, Tink, it's *supposed* to be a punishment," he snarled, rubbing her knot faster.

She scowled back at him, but it was quickly replaced with a gasp and a moan when he pushed his cock into her wet pussy.

"Ohhh," they groaned in unison, and he lifted her off the nonslip floor to deepen the penetration. She wrapped her arms around his neck and her legs around his waist, and he began fucking her against the shower wall.

He thrust in and out of her, her back thumping against the wall and her boobs bouncing with every push.

"Fuck, you feel good," he panted.

She began to murmur dirty words in his ear. Words that would normally make her blush, but frankly, she was feeling self-conscious about how heavy she had to be and wanted him to come soon. She knew he liked it when she talked dirty.

"Oh my god, Jake. Your cock feels so good inside my pussy. Fuck me, baby. Fuck me like I'm your whore."

He began to grunt and pound her harder, so she continued.

"I want you to come deep inside me. Please. I want to feel your cum dripping out of my pussy, baby."

He threw his head back and groaned, "Ohhh fuuuck," then slammed into her at a furious pace. Suddenly he pulled her down on his cock so he was fully seated inside and let out a low growl as she felt his spurts of cum deep inside her like she'd begged for.

Damn, did it feel sexy, and she was really turned on, and a little disappointed with herself for pushing him over the edge so quickly. Especially since he was still holding her like she weighed nothing.

Jake slowly lowered her to the ground, warm water spraying on them. He pulled the showerhead from its holder, and brought it between her legs to clean her.

A soft mewl escaped her lips when the jets hit her clit, and a grin crossed his lips.

"You like that, baby?"

She bit her bottom lip and nodded.

"Spread your legs, Tink."

She did as he instructed, leaning back against the wall for support as Jacob pulled the hood of her clit back and let the jets do their magic.

It was the fastest orgasm of her life, even quicker than when she was with BOB—her battery operated boyfriend. Like her climaxes with BOB, it wasn't the most fulfilling, but it got the job done. Taren knew she was in store for better, later.

Jake kissed her softly, then pressed the button to cease the water while he pumped shampoo from the wall dispenser into his hand. As he moved to lather her hair with it, she was going to correct him and tell him she had her own special shampoo, but thought better of it and just accepted the loving act instead.

He then thoroughly rinsed her hair, concentrating to make sure he didn't miss any spots, and dropped another kiss on her lips with a satisfied smile, which she easily returned. How could she not? A sexy, gorgeous man was naked in the shower with her, in the middle of an expensive vacation that he'd surprised her with, washing her hair. *Hello, dream life.*

He quickly lathered his body while she watched, mesmerized. He was so incredibly sexy, watching his muscles move as he washed his chest made her catch her breath. It took him less than thirty seconds to shampoo his short hair, then reached for the taps as the water streamed down his face before he shut them off.

He wrapped a white towel around her first before grabbing one from the shelf for himself.

As he dried his legs, he looked up at her with a grin. "Wanna get married today?"

"My answer is the same as when you asked yesterday. And the day before."

"Just checking. One day, you'll say yes. All I can do is ask, right?"

She rolled her eyes but a grin escaped her lips.

"And for the record," he said as he wrapped the towel around his waist, his Adonis belt making her mouth water. "I didn't ask yesterday; I didn't see you yesterday."

"Well, whose fault is that?" she teased. "Yesterday might have been the day I would have said yes." She winced like the words pained her. "I guess we'll never know."

The look he gave her sent shivers down her spine.

"Keep talking, little one. You're not going to be able to sit down for a week."

Why she felt the need to poke the bear, she'd never know, but she did.

"I don't know... I've got a lot of padding back here," she said, patting her bum over the towel tucked around her as she walked out of the bathroom.

He reached for her wrist and drew her back to him, wrapping his arm around her and snaking his hand under the fabric to grab a handful of flesh from her bottom and jiggled it like he was measuring it with his palm.

"I'd say it's just the right amount."

She rolled her eyes again.

"And it's going to be such a nice shade of red later," he smirked.

Taren tried to shrug it off like she wasn't concerned as she pulled away from him, but inside her stomach was doing flip flops with excitement.

****

Jacob

Funny what a difference a week makes.

Last Thursday, he was in Abu Dhabi, tying up loose ends on a project in anticipation of being gone on his cruise with Taren for ten days—his first vacation in seven years. Not even in his most hopeful dreams had he thought he'd be in the shower, naked with her a week later.

Now, Jacob was days away from possibly having her in his house, forever. He just needed to play his cards right and determine the right amount to push—not an easy feat.

But knowing how to handle every situation was his specialty and how he earned the big bucks. Hopefully his heart didn't cloud his judgment.

Chapter Twenty-Three

Taren

Their remaining time on board could only be described as perfect. Between the gourmet food, the time by the pool, the time spent over his knee and in his bed...

"Can people die from happiness?" she wondered out loud as she draped herself on his lap on the couch in an attempt to distract him from work on their last afternoon at sea. Tomorrow morning, they would be getting off the ship and back to reality. What that reality looked like, they'd carefully avoided discussing.

He promptly closed his laptop, like he always did when she was near his screen, and brought his arms around her, tucking his chin on her shoulder.

"I've heard of people dying from a broken heart, but from happiness? Absolutely not."

"I can understand someone dying from a broken heart," she murmured. "Been there. Never want to do that again, thank you very much."

"I agree. Which is why I think we need to stop in Houston and pack your things and move you to New Orleans with me, tomorrow."

Taren knew this conversation was coming and had made up her mind about what she wanted to do.

She turned her body and cupped his cheek. "I can't, Jake."

He didn't even try to disguise his displeasure, but said nothing until she grinned, "I have to give my work two weeks' notice, and let East Jefferson know I'll accept their job offer, before I can leave."

He dipped her onto the couch, snarling, "You little minx!" then smiled down on her before kissing her softly. "So, you wanna get married today?"

Someday soon, she was going to call his bluff. Just not today, in case he really wasn't pretending. Deep down, she knew he was serious.

"Not today, but thank you for asking."

His phone dinged, and he looked at her solemnly. "Why don't you go to the pool? I don't want you waiting around for me. I really need to deal with this. It's important."

Based on the look on his face, Taren knew it must be.

"Okay," she said softly, and he moved to let her up. "Everything okay?" she asked from the doorway leading to her cabin.

"No, Tink. It's not. I'm worried something big is about to happen in Ensenada, and I'm trying to figure out which sources to believe."

"Oh." She didn't know what else to say. "Anything I can do to help?"

He shook his head as he opened his computer back up. "I'm afraid not. Just be patient with me as I try to get this worked out."

"Of course, baby. I'll just be reading by the pool. Can I get you to put sunscreen on my back before I go, though?"

"Sure," he said, no longer looking at her but at something on his screen. "Put your suit on and I'll be happy to."

"Thanks," she said before disappearing into her room. She could tell he was really concerned about whatever it was he was dealing with. She hoped Bella and Dante and their little girl were going to be okay. In that short afternoon she'd spent with them, she'd gotten to really like them—especially Bella and her sister. They had treated her with such kindness. And their daughters were too beautiful for words. Little Madison had been something else—her crush on Jacob was adorable.

She returned with a bottle of sunscreen, and Jacob reluctantly closed his laptop as she approached, his brows furrowed with unease.

"It's very important that you don't talk to anyone you've not spoken to before or to someone you don't recognize as seeing around during this trip, Tink," he said as he rubbed the lotion on her back. "Make sure you're only drinking unopened bottled water or you watch your bartender make your drink. And take your bag with the phone in it, okay?"

"Yeah, of course," she said compliantly. The fact that he was so troubled had her worried. He was normally cool as a cucumber. This must be bad.

"Keep your phone on, baby. I'll try to check on you about every half hour. Just let me know if you decide to get in the pool, that way I won't worry if you don't answer."

"O—o—okay," she stuttered. "Would you rather I just stay here?"

She watched him will a smile on his face and try to soften his body language.

"No, go enjoy your day. I'm sure I'm just being overly vigilant. But be aware of your surroundings, okay?"

"I will," she promised.

Grabbing her multi-colored beach bag, she put the phone, sunscreen, her Kindle, and two bottles of water in it, then headed to the Lido deck. Her mind filled with worry.

****

Jacob

The underground was buzzing about a band of men from Los Zetas being in Ensenada—a long way from their territory on the west side of Mexico. There was also chatter that there were Colombians there too; but those sources were less reliable. Jacob was reaching out to his network to see if he could get the real story.

Any way he sliced it, nothing good could come from Zetas being in the Sinaloans' domain.

Jacob was upset to be missing out on the last day of his cruise with Tink, and he hated sending her to the pool by herself. He was especially annoyed with himself for alarming her that anything was wrong, but he wanted her to be vigilant. Plus, he felt like he needed to at least offer an explanation why he wasn't joining her today. She seemed to understand.

Speaking of... he needed to check on her. He'd put a tracker on her phone and another in her big bag, but they only worked if she had those items in her possession. Texting her was an option, but since they hadn't established a code word before she left, it could be anyone replying to him. He needed to call her. Better yet, he decided to take a thirty-minute break and go sit with her.

He changed into board shorts and a t-shirt, then slipped on some flip flops and aviator sunglasses. At the last second, he grabbed his phone—just in case one of his contacts decided to reach out to him, then headed out to find his girl. He was sure she was spreading her fairy dust all over the Lido deck that very moment.

Instead, he found her in a lounge chair with a floppy hat and sunglasses, reading her Kindle and not chatting with anyone. Rather than approaching her, he went to the bar and ordered a Scotch on the rocks for him and that fruity frozen drink she'd been enjoying all week.

She glanced up when he sat down in the lounger next to her, and broke into a big smile.

"Hi! I didn't expect to see you here!"

He handed her the red drink.

"I decided to take a little break and hang out with my favorite fairy. Maybe go for a swim before heading back."

"Did you get everything figured out?"

"No. Still working on it. I have a feeling I'm going to be heading to Ensenada after I drop you off in Houston."

She nodded thoughtfully.

"I wish there was something I could do to help."

He reached behind and pulled his t-shirt over his head, then sat back on the lounger and picked up his drink.

"Just being understanding helps me a lot. I can't worry about you being mad at me and deal with this mess."

"Of course I understand." She gave him a seductive grin. "But if you're going to be out in the sun, you should probably put sunscreen on. Lie on your stomach, and I'll get your back for you."

Having her hands on him was exactly what he needed. She seemed to sense it too, because she took a long time caressing his back, then even applied lotion on his arms and the backs of his legs, talking softly the whole time.

"I think you need a massage, baby."

"Fuck that," he growled. "Like I trust anyone enough to do that."

"I could do it."

He did like what she was currently doing to him.

"Yeah?" he asked, raising his head slightly to look at her.

"Why not? You give me massages; I'd be happy to return the favor."

"Do I get a happy ending?" he teased.

She discreetly slipped her hand up his shorts and cupped his balls, murmuring, "Do you even need to ask?"

"God, I love you, Tink."

"Mmm, feeling's mutual, baby," she whispered in his ear as she moved her hands up to his shoulders and rubbed her tits against his back.

"Keep that up, and we're going back to the cabin."

With her lips on his cheek, she giggled, "That's the plan, silly."

His phone alerted, and he groaned as he sat up to look at the message.

With a sigh, he closed his eyes and drooped his shoulders. "I have to go." After slipping his t-shirt back on, he leaned over and, with his hand entwined in her hair at the back of her head, kissed her like he meant it; not caring about the PDA or what anyone else thought.

"This will be continued later," he growled, draining his drink and setting it back on the table before standing up.

She put her hand at her forehead to block the sun as she looked up at him.

"Are you coming back?"

"I'll try, but don't count on it. We will have dinner later though, I promise."

Taren stroked the back of his calf tenderly when she asked, "Have you even eaten lunch?"

"No. Have you?"

"No. How about I bring us something in about an hour?"

Jacob dropped a kiss on her forehead, telling her, "Thanks, Tink. I'd appreciate that," then headed back to his suite. He had a feeling he wasn't about to get good news.

Chapter Twenty-Four

Taren

She slipped quietly into her cabin, carrying a tray with two turkey paninis, French fries, and sodas, and set it down at her table, where she unloaded the dishes and tried to make it look as inviting as she could. Walking into his room, she found him on his phone, pacing.

"I need you to send me that intel the second you have it confirmed," he instructed the caller on the other end. "And you need to get a new burner phone. Call me on the backup number; I'm going to lose this one as soon as I make one more call."

He hung up, then started punching buttons on his phone, so she knocked on the door frame to get his attention.

"Hey, I brought lunch."

Jacob looked up from the phone in his hand at her and hesitated before walking over and hugging her around her shoulders. It felt very obligatory.

"I've just got to make this one call, and I'll be right over."

"Okay. It's paninis and fries, so, it might get cold," she warned.

"Don't wait for me, but this shouldn't take long."

"Oh, okay."

As she stepped back to her side of the door, he closed it behind her. It was the first time since he opened it the second day of the cruise that the wooden barrier had been shut. It felt ominous, and she wanted to wrench it back open. Not because she wanted to listen to his conversation, but because the closed door between them seemed symbolic somehow, and she didn't like it one bit.

Taren sat down at the table and picked at her lunch. It had smelled so good when she carried it to her cabin, excited to have lunch with Jake. Staring at the empty chair across from her as she took a bite, it no longer had any appeal. Even the fries that had seemed to have the perfect amount of crispness to them as she ate a few on her way, now tasted soggy and cold.

After thirty minutes, she pushed away from the table, set the tray of uneaten food outside her cabin door, gathered her beach bag, and returned to the pool to try to get lost in a book and not think about Jake. She knew what was happening was not personal, and it had to be important for him to blow her off like that, but still, her feelings were a little hurt.

The cruise ship had those great reading chairs with a face cradle, similar to ones massage therapists used, so she was lying on her stomach reading when she dozed off. Next thing she knew, she felt someone's hands applying lotion to her shoulders and she jumped, turning onto her side in the process.

"It's just me, Tink," Jacob's deep voice reassured her. "You were getting pink." He leaned closer to her ear, "I'm the only one who's supposed to make your skin pink, and not on your shoulders."

She laid back on her stomach and let him finish reapplying sunscreen.

"My cabana boy has been neglecting me today."

"I know, baby, I'm sorry. I promise it's not because I wanted to."

His fingertips traced her side boob up and down.

"I can reach there," she scolded him even as her nipples pebbled at his touch.

"Are you sure? You wouldn't want to get sunburned there. I better make sure you have adequate coverage."

"Well, if you think it's necessary…"

"Oh, it's very necessary." He lathered sunscreen on the skin peeking out of the side of her bathing suit top. She felt his pinkie finger slip under the triangle shaped fabric and trace over her stiff nipple. "My poor little fairy has been neglected today. I promise I will make it up to you."

"How?" she challenged.

"However you want."

She turned to face the other direction. "Hmm, let me think about it."

He bent over her so he could discreetly tweak her nipple with two fingers.

"Don't get cocky, little one, or your ass will match your shoulders."

****

Jacob

"I figured out how you can make it up to me," Taren said from the lounger next to him.

He pulled his sunglasses down his nose to look at her suspiciously. "How?"

"I want to go dancing tonight."

She *knew* he didn't dance and was taking advantage of his feeling guilty for ignoring her and missing lunch. The lunch that she had thoughtfully brought back just for him that ended up getting thrown out because he was caught up in trying to determine what the hell Los Zetas were doing in Ensenada before it was too late.

Ramon had already returned to California, and Dante decided he was taking Bella and Madison to John's place in San Diego in the morning.

Right now, the Guzmans had scouts out looking for the interlopers while Jacob was pulling out all the stops with his underground contacts. The problem was, the Zetas were notoriously ruthless with their enemies, so it was harder to get people to talk. Money wasn't the incentive it usually was; people couldn't spend money when their headless bodies were hanging from a bridge.

Until Jacob heard something from his network, his hands were tied. It looked like he was taking Taren to the nightclub after dinner.

"Dancing, huh? What made you decide that?"

"Because any other time you'd say no."

"That's not true. Anytime you want to go, all you have to do is ask. I'll be happy to take you."

"I want to go dancing tonight," she retorted.

"Then that's what we're doing," he said with a placating smile.

"And you have to act like you're having a good time."

"Baby, anytime that I'm spending with you is a good time."

That was the truth. He'd do just about anything if it made her happy. He fucking lived to make her happy.

She smiled and reached for his hand.

"It'll be fun," she assured him. "Just consider it one of our many adventures."

"Now you're just being patronizing. I suggest you tread lightly."

"Or what?"

He put his sunglasses on his head and looked at her. He hadn't put her over his knee since Friday—it was now Wednesday. It dawned on him that she was purposefully trying to earn a punishment.

"That's Strike Two, Tinkerbell," he warned with a raised eyebrow, just in case he was wrong.

"Well your entire side struck out this afternoon, so you don't have any room to talk," she sassed back with her arms folded across her chest.

He quietly gathered their things and put them in the colorful bag she'd brought with her, then stood and offered her his hand.

"I think you've had too much sun, baby. You don't appear to be thinking straight. Let's go."

Chapter Twenty-Five

Taren

She'd been thinking about being disciplined ever since he showed up and told her he was the only one who was supposed to make her skin pink. Then he sat down on the lounge chair next to her and made no further mention of it.

So, a girl's gotta do what a girl's gotta do.

Part of her was happy to behave like a brat. She'd been feeling resentful about being ignored today. Logically, she knew she had no right to be upset—he was attending to important business, but emotionally, well, that was another story. Acting out was a nice release, and she was going to be put over his knee for it. Win-win.

They walked into her cabin, and he closed the door then threw the security lock before striding to the couch and sitting down without a word. Taren busied herself looking through her bag, pretending to be oblivious that she had a spanking coming.

"Tinkerbell," he said authoritatively.

"Hmm?" she said, refusing to avert her attention from the phantom item she was busy searching her bag for.

"Taren Scarlett Fairchild, look at me."

Slowly, she drew her eyes to his. *Dammit*, those green eyes and cheekbones turned her to mush every time.

"Come here," he growled softly and held his hand out as she slowly started walking toward him. When she was within his reach, he circled her wrist in his grip and drew her into his lap.

"I haven't taken very good care of you today, have I?"

"No, you haven't," she pouted, looking down and fighting back tears. His acknowledging he'd neglected her filled her with self-pity and made her want to cry.

"Is that why you're being so sassy? Are you trying to get my attention?"

When he put it like that, he made her feel like a three-year-old. Still... he was probably onto something.

"No," she said defiantly.

He put a knuckle under her chin and raised it to look at him. With a quirked eyebrow, he asked, "No?"

"I don't know. Maybe."

"Tell me what you need, baby."

She wasn't going to say she needed him to take charge and manhandle her, even if that's what she was secretly craving.

"I don't need anything from you," she huffed.

A slow smile of realization formed on his lips.

"Oh, I think you do."

****

Jacob

Her defiance spoke volumes.

Lifting her off his lap, he stood her in front of him and casually looked her up and down from head to toe. She was so beautiful. Her sun-kissed skin and platinum blonde hair a sexy contrast to the black bikini she was currently clad in under the see-through white netting that was supposed to be considered her 'bathing suit cover-up'. It was more like a fucking dick tease.

Without warning, he ripped it down the center as she gasped in surprise, then yanked her black bottoms to her knees and forcefully put her over his knee, ass up as he sat back down.

She didn't put up a fight. On the contrary, she raised her bottom for him as she mewled softly with her face in the couch cushion. He'd bet his bank account she was soaked.

"I think you need to be punished, little one. As a matter of fact, I think you *want* to be punished."

She didn't object, just lie there with her ass in the air, wiggling it slightly in invitation.

He rubbed her soft flesh in wide circles with both hands and squeezed firmly, before landing the first hit to her left cheek. It was a quick whack, followed by a succession of smacks alternating between the left and right. Her skin immediately began to transform to a beautiful shade of red. Jacob didn't stop until she began to squirm in his lap.

He dipped his hand between her legs and up her slit.

"You're drenched," he chuckled. He'd intended for it come out sternly, but he couldn't help himself. He loved that she was turned on.

She pressed against his hand, and he grabbed a fistful of her hair.

"What do you think you're doing?" he hissed. This time, he was able to channel his inner Dom.

"I'm sorry, Sir!"

"Not yet, but you're going to be."

He rained down more blows while sliding two fingers inside her pussy.

Jacob paused with his hand in midair when he felt her cunt tighten around his digits, and warned, "Don't you dare come while I'm spanking you."

She let out a mangled cry and scraped her fingers along the cushions, seeking purchase. Finding none, she hit the couch with the palm of her hand and bucked her hips up in frustration before collapsing back over his lap like a ragdoll.

Chuckling to himself, he rubbed her ass firmly instead of spanking it and halted his finger fucking to a teasing pace. The only sounds in the room were her whimpers and his fingers slowly moving in and out of her pussy.

His cock was so fucking hard it was pressing against her thighs on his lap. By the way she was squirming, she knew how turned on he was.

"Please," she whispered.

Jake started to trace the crack of her ass with his other hand, dipping into her pussy and spreading her juices to her star.

"Please what?"

"Please fuck me."

He pushed the tip of his ring finger into her ass, leisurely moving it to match the pace of his finger in her pussy.

"Where do you want me to fuck you, Tinkerbell?"

"Ohhh," she moaned, widening her legs. "Wherever you want, Sir. I love it when you use me for your pleasure."

His cock was leaking now.

Jacob plunged his fingers deep inside both holes, and Taren let out a low, muffled moan as she started to come undone right before him. It was so fucking sexy.

"What did I say about coming?" he barked, even as he fucked her pussy and ass faster, drawing her orgasm from her.

She unapologetically rocked against his hand until she clenched so tight he couldn't move his fingers anymore, then it was like someone opened floodgates and her whole body relaxed before she began shuddering in his lap, moaning in ecstasy.

As she lie panting, her bikini bottoms now around one ankle, and his dick hard as steel, his phone dinged.

Goddammit. Although he was thankful it hadn't gone off two minutes earlier.

Jacob gingerly lifted her off his lap and scooped her up to lay her down on the bed.

"Do you have to answer that?" she asked quietly.

He glanced down to see it was from Jesus Gutierrez, one of his most trusted sources in Mexico and Central America.

"I do."

She nodded in understanding, then pointedly looked down at his cock still tenting his swim trunks.

"That's a shame. I was really looking forward to sucking on that."

He bit back a groan. If this had involved the safety of anyone other than Bella and Dante, and more importantly, their daughter, he might have taken her up on the blowjob before tending to business. But he actually cared about the Guzmans, especially their little girl—not a usual occurrence for him.

"Hold that thought," he grumbled as he retreated to his cabin with his phone in his hand.

He sat down at the table and opened his laptop to download the photos Jesus had sent him along with intelligence reports when she appeared in the doorway—wearing nothing but a pair of sexy as fuck heels.

Strutting toward him with a smug smile, she commented, "I'd rather hold something else," then dropped to her knees to the side of his chair. He spun the seat so she was directly between his legs and lifted his ass slightly to help when she began to tug on his shorts, while maneuvering his computer screen on the table away from her field of vision.

Not that she was looking at his laptop.

Her gasp when his cock sprang free from his shorts fed his ego, as did her soft moan of "ohhh," before she reverently rubbed his cock against her cheeks with her eyes closed.

He glanced at the screen and clicked a few buttons to start the download process, then sat back and watched her take his cock between her lips. Looking up at him with a seductive smile, she took him all the way down—every inch, until her nose was pressed against his hips.

The little gagging noise she made before looking up at him again with watery eyes made him want to grab her hair and face fuck her. Instead he closed his eyes and stroked her hair.

"That's a good girl," he cooed.

Jacob opened his eyes to find hers fixed on his face. He observed in awe as she began to work her hand in unison with her mouth while maintaining eye contact with him. His little fairy had morphed into a sultry siren right before his eyes.

Damn, she was beautiful. And she was *his*.

Unable to help himself, he threw his head back and closed his eyes, relishing how good she was making him feel.

"I thought you needed to work?" she smirked as she stroked him up and down.

He opened his eyes and slammed the lid of his laptop closed without even looking at it.

"It can wait."

Watching her suck his cock like a goddamn porn star, it wasn't going to have to wait long, and he began to moan his impending release.

"Come on my face," she whispered.

"Fuuuuck!" he groaned while standing up and jerking his cock, aiming it for her pretty face as she looked up at him with those big blue eyes, her hands on his thighs.

She closed her eyes when he began to paint her face. There wasn't a full tank, so to speak, since she'd been emptying him several times a day for the past ten days. Then she reached up and smeared it across her skin and lips, and he growled—literally.

"Fuck, you are sexy."

"You make me feel sexy," she whispered and stood up, retreating to the bathroom. Moments later, she came out wiping a hand towel across her face.

"I'll let you get back to work now," she smirked.

Holding his hand out, he commanded, "Come here."

She did as he asked, and he pulled her into his lap, putting his arms around her waist and his chin on her shoulder,

"I'm sorry for neglecting you today. I'll make it up to you, I promise."

She turned slightly so she was looking at him and cupped his cheek. "You already have," she said in a low voice, then softly kissed his lips.

Jacob dropped his forehead to hers and closed his eyes.

"I love you, Tink."

"I love you, too, J.P."

A corner of his mouth turned up.

"J.P.?"

Taren stood up and starting walking toward the door.

"Yeah, your initials? Jacob Preston?"

"I know what they stand for; you've just never called me that."

"Well, for a while there, it stood for jerky prick. I'm happy they mean something else now."

"What do they mean now?"

She winked at him. "You've got work to do," then closed the door behind her.

He did have work to do, otherwise, he'd barge into her cabin and demand she answer him. He sat wracking his brain as he opened his computer back up; something he suspected was her plan.

The documents and photos grabbed his attention, and he ceased trying to figure out what J.P. meant until later. He'd get it out of her—one way or another.

Chapter Twenty-Six

Taren

She'd really meant she was just happy his initials stood for his name again and not *jerky prick*, but now Jacob thought she'd assigned new meaning to them. She'd have to come up with something clever, but not right now. Her brain was barely functioning after their most recent sexscapade.

Taren went to bed, fully expecting he'd show up sometime in the middle of the night and hold her, but at the moment, she was content knowing he was on the other side of the door.

Like she'd predicted, he came to bed around three a.m., but lasted less than ninety minutes. She only knew he left because he tripped over her suitcase she'd packed the night before in preparation of debarking in San Diego later that morning.

"Everything okay?" she said in the darkness.

"Yeah, I'm sorry to wake you, baby. Just stubbed my toe."

She glanced at the time on the clock on the nightstand and sat up, switching on the lamp and pulling the covers to her chest.

"No, I mean is *everything* okay. You didn't even sleep for two hours."

He looked haggard when he sat down on the bed next to her.

"No. I'm going to have to get off the ship the second it docks and fly to Ensenada. Madison is missing."

It felt like all the blood just rushed to her feet, and her heart was pounding in her ears. Surely, she misheard him.

"What do you mean, 'Madison is missing?' How can she be missing?"

"Two of Dante's guards were found murdered, and she was not in her room or anywhere on the property after they turned it upside down looking for her."

"Do they have any idea who took her?"

"Yeah. They're just waiting for the ransom request, in addition to the entire city being on the lookout for her. If she's still alive, they'll find her. There's no way they're getting her out of the city. The Guzmans are loved by everyone in that town—cops, criminals, and common people."

"*If* she's still alive..." Taren felt like vomiting. She could only imagine the anguish Bella and Dante had to be going through.

He put his arm around her and hugged her tight, which triggered her tears.

"That sweet little girl—how could someone do such a thing?"

"She's alive, baby. They're not going to hurt her. Not yet, anyway. But we're racing against the clock. And there's only so much I can do on this goddamn boat."

"You need to try to sleep a little more," she suggested. "You're going to want a clear head when we get to Ensenada."

"*We*?" he said with a grin. "Nice try, little one. You're going back to Houston and giving your notice. I've already upgraded your flight. I can't have you in Mexico; I'd be distracted, worrying about you, too."

She wanted to argue, but didn't think her presence in Ensenada would have brought anything to the table. It wasn't like Dante and Bella needed her to make them a casserole for dinner or pick up some groceries—things she'd normally do for a friend in crisis. She'd just be in the way.

"I get it. Let's talk in an hour, okay? I'll set my alarm for five-thirty. You really need some more rest. It's not good for you to go on such little sleep."

He must have been really tired, because he reluctantly returned to bed next to her. She switched off the lamp, and wrapped her arms around his middle, knowing she wasn't going to fall asleep but hoping Jake at least dozed off. He needed it.

It was impossible not to wonder who these people were that took Madi. Would her and Jacob's children be in danger someday, too?

She loved Jacob, but this... this was making her pause. Maybe being with him meant they shouldn't have children. That thought made her heart heavy; she wanted children— and her clock was ticking. Her doctor had told her she should try to be done having her babies by thirty-six; it was one of the many catalysts to spur her to divorce David. She didn't have time to waste.

The soft snoring of Jacob brought her back to the present, and she watched him sleep, fighting the urge to caress his face. He was a light sleeper—lighter than anyone she'd ever known. The slightest touch, and he'd be awake. Learning what he did for a living helped clear up why.

He was such a beautiful man, with his long eyelashes and high cheekbones... not to mention his incredible physique. Taren really had no idea what he was doing with her. She was cute—at best, certainly not model-worthy like he was. Yet, he somehow always managed to make her feel like the most beautiful girl in the room.

With a sigh, her thoughts returned to Bella and Dante and what they had to be feeling. She couldn't even begin to imagine their torment, because when she tried, she was right back to wondering if being with Jacob was the right thing to do if she wanted to be a mother someday soon.

Chapter Twenty-Seven

Jacob

The Sinaloans seemed to think it was the Colombians who took Madison Guzman, and were focusing on locating them. He knew that was bullshit. Los Zetas were responsible; he was sure of it. The underground chatter of a group of them being in Ensenada couldn't have been a coincidence; there'd been radio silence about any South American cartel in Sinaloa. Unfortunately, the Zetas had done a bang up job of framing the Colombians, and Dante was convinced his daughter was on a cargo ship headed to Cartagena, despite Jacob trying to convince him otherwise.

"What the fuck did my million dollars buy, Jacob?" he'd accused in the early morning hours while Jake was still at sea. "It bought dick. It bought me being placated into thinking they'd agreed to a truce only to turn around and snatch my baby girl from her bed."

"Dante, with all due respect, I think you need to refocus. Think about it. Los Zetas would have a lot to gain if you went to war with the Colombians. Intelligence is telling me—"

"I don't give a goddamn about your intelligence!" the Mexican roared. "If your fucking *intelligence* is so great, why don't they know where the fuck my daughter is?"

Jacob knew the man was distraught, and there was no point trying to reason with him when he was in this state of mind. Especially over the phone.

"I'm on a plane the second the ship docks in a few hours."

"I'll see you then," Dante said in clipped tones, hanging up without another word.

He'd needed to sleep. Actually, what he'd needed was to hold Tink, so he crawled into bed with her. He hadn't planned on telling her about Madison, but then realized the kidnapping had the potential to make international news. She'd never forgive him if she learned of Madi's abduction from Channel 13 News. When she woke up after he kicked her suitcase, and she questioned how everything was going, it seemed to be the best opportunity. Telling her actually took some of the weight off his shoulders. He'd been trying to figure out how he was going to explain putting her in a first-class seat back to Houston alone, while he headed elsewhere. When she suggested he return to bed with her, he did it only to placate her worry about him getting enough rest and fully expected to lie there with his wheels turning until she fell back asleep. Apparently, that wasn't the case.

****

He knew he was dreaming. His subconscious was telling him that, as if to allow his brain to continue the process. He could see Madison but couldn't seem to reach her—every time he took a step toward her, she seemed to get further away so he stopped trying and just watched. It was as though they were in a vast warehouse—there were no windows and the only light was from a single bulb above the little girl's head. She was sitting on the concrete floor, surrounded by walls of colorful blankets, t-shirts, and purses, and she seemed completely oblivious, playing with piles of ceramic magnets in a jumble of colors like the selection Taren had purchased.

The toddler crashed two tortoise shaped ones together, causing them to crack. That's when she looked around, realized she was alone, and started to cry. Madison reached out toward him, but this time he couldn't even walk toward her—he was waist high in mud as faceless people came out from behind the piles of goods surrounding her, offering other toys as consolation. She refused everything until someone offered her what appeared to be a bomb that was beeping softly.

The beeping got louder. And louder. Until...

A familiar hand was on his shoulder, soft lips brushing against his ear.

"Baby, it's time to wake up."

The beeping stopped and his eyes flew open, and he looked around the room, trying to orient himself.

He must have looked confused—or terrified, because Taren sat down on the bed next to him and brushed his hair behind his ear.

"Are you okay?"

"No," he said, scrubbing the stubble on his chin with his hand. "I had a terrible nightmare about Madison."

"Oh, babe. You said so yourself, she's still alive and in Ensenada. I know it doesn't mean anything, but I think you're right. I feel it in my heart that she's still okay."

Or maybe it's just wishful thinking.

He didn't say that—he didn't want to be a dick and piss on her good feelings, and he also didn't want to voice his fear, as if actually saying it out loud would somehow lend it credence. He wasn't necessarily a believer in all the woo-woo stuff that Taren believed in; putting shit out into the universe, blah blah blah, but he wasn't risking it right now either.

"I dreamed she was in an endless warehouse, filled with all that crap the street vendors in Ensenada sell—tchotchkes, t-shirts, purses, blankets."

She took a deep breath as she contemplated that.

"Well, maybe that's where you should start looking."

"Where? Warehouses or street vendors?"

She made a pained face. "I don't know? Both?"

"Because I had a dream?"

She shrugged. "It could also just mean you think she's still in the city, and those things represent Ensenada to you."

He stood and kissed her on the forehead.

"You've been a huge help, Tink."

"For future reference—just in case you need it someday—sarcasm at six in the morning, or really any time before coffee, is grounds for divorce."

"Noted."

He walked into his cabin to start packing and stopped short, then slowly walked back through the door to hers.

"You packed my things?"

She scrunched up her nose and started talking faster than normal.

"I hope that's okay? I wanted to let you sleep a little longer, so I thought if I packed your suitcase, all you would have to do is shower and get your work stuff together. I promise I didn't touch your computer or anything that remotely looked like business. Just your clothes and stuff. I left your toiletries out."

"That was... that was really thoughtful. Thanks, baby."

He got in the shower, unsure how he really felt about her getting his suitcase ready. He knew the gesture came from a good place, but he'd been fiercely independent for a long time. He hadn't had anyone take care of him like that since... well, Taren. Seven years ago. She'd never packed his bags then, but she had been known to pack a lunch, grab his hand, and tell him she was taking him on a picnic. Or how she'd buy him a shirt when she was out shopping because she thought the color would look good with his eyes, or some shit, and have it waiting for him the next time he came into town. Not to mention all the times he'd find a sentimental card in his bag when he got home or a love note tucked in a pocket.

He'd forgotten what that was like—how good it made him feel to have her little acts of love in his life.

He never wanted to lose that again. He didn't know what he'd do if something ever happened to her. With Madi's disappearance, he was genuinely worried about Taren's safety, yet he couldn't be in two places at once. Exactly the feelings he'd had seven years ago when he ended things with her. Time and distance had made him forget, but here he was again.

****

Taren

Jacob wanted to drop her off at the airport on his way to the private runway.

"I'm sorry I can't fly you to Houston like I'd originally planned," he said as their Uber driver pulled up to the area marked departures. "But I upgraded your ticket to first class. It's important that you call me with this phone"—he handed her a new phone—"when you land and when you get home."

"Okay, I will," she said softly.

She pecked him on the cheek and turned to get out of the vehicle when he hauled her back against him, kissing her thoroughly as the driver got out to retrieve her luggage from the trunk. She clung to him as the realization this would be their last kiss for a while washed over her, and when he finally broke the kiss, she wasn't ready.

"Come on," he said with a sad smile and opened his car door to get out with her.

They stood on the sidewalk, neither seeming to want to say goodbye, even though the driver was back in the car waiting for him now, having deposited her suitcase on the sidewalk.

"How long before you come to Houston?"

"I'm not sure, baby. Given the circumstance…"

She knew he couldn't say anything more in front of other passengers walking by.

"I understand. I'll talk to you in a couple of hours. Give Bella and Dante a hug for me." Taren stood on her tiptoes and kissed his cheek again, whispering in his ear, "Find her, Jake," before dropping to the balls of her feet and pulling up the telescopic luggage handle.

"I will, I promise," he said, then grabbed her elbow, looking into her eyes. "You need to be extra vigilant—do you understand me? If *anything* feels off, you need to trust your gut and go somewhere where there's a lot of people, then call me. I mean it, Taren."

"You're scaring me, Jake."

"Good. This is important."

She nodded as her mind raced. She didn't like this one bit.

He leaned down and kissed her below her ear, whispering. "I love you, Tinkerbell. Don't forget to call me. I'll wait until you're inside."

She smiled meekly then turned to walk through the automatic sliding glass doors; her stomach in knots. This wasn't at all how she'd envisioned flying back to Houston was going to be like.

****

Pulling her luggage through her tiny apartment door, it felt like the last ten days had been a dream, and she was finally waking up again as the familiarity of her life in Houston came rushing back.

She had been in her new place only a few months, but it was long enough that she'd acclimated.

Crap. If she moved to New Orleans, she was going to have to break her lease.

What an odd thing to consider at a time like this.

But it had been actually been in the 'cons' column when she made out her list of pros and cons after getting the job offer and couldn't decide what to do. Obviously, now at the top of the 'pros' list was Jacob Preston Smith. But her safety could be on the cons side.

Taren called the number programmed in the phone he'd given her, as he'd requested, and it went straight to a generic voicemail, just like it had when she'd called him after landing at George Bush Intercontinental.

"Hey, it's me. Just calling again—like you asked me to. I made it home okay. Hope you made it to Ensenada safely and Madi is already home. I love you. Call me when you can— don't worry about what time it is. I want to talk to you; I don't care if that means waking me up. I love you. I already said that. Okay, well… hope to talk to you soon."

She needed to keep busy and decided to unpack and do laundry, and get her clothes ready for work tomorrow. It didn't take much, she wore scrubs, but it was always a good idea to make sure she had a clean set for the next day rather than getting up in the morning and discovering she had none. That was how she'd acquired so many—more than once she'd stopped to buy a new pair on her way to work because she didn't have a clean set.

With a sigh, she realized she was also going to have to put in her notice soon. Not tomorrow, the day she returned from a ten-day vacation after being on the job less than six months, that would be the ultimate in bad form. But soon. Besides, she needed to confirm everything with East Jefferson first and make sure the job offer still stood.

It was going to be a busy day tomorrow, and thankfully a long one. Hopefully the twelve-hour shift would keep her mind off Jacob and Madi.

She flipped on the ten o'clock news while skimming the headlines on her tablet. No mention of little Madison Guzman being kidnapped—anywhere. She even clicked on the Ensenada newspaper on her tablet. Her Spanish wasn't that great, but she knew enough to know what their news stories were about and none were of a three-year-old little girl being abducted.

Taren didn't know if the lack of news coverage was a good or bad thing. Jacob hadn't called her back, so all she could was wait. And hopefully not go crazy with worry in the meantime.

Chapter Twenty-Eight

Jacob

The scene at the Guzman estate could best be described as highly secured chaos. The guards around the estate had been tripled, there were two helicopters on the grounds—Ramon's and the new one John had been using to fly back and forth between Ensenada and his home in San Diego.

Understandably, Dante looked like shit. Not surprisingly, Bella looked like she was ready to kick ass—she just needed to be pointed in the right direction. Edward and Reagan were there—their baby, Brianna, noticeably wasn't.

"We decided it would be better if she stayed in South Dakota," Edward explained when Jacob inquired where she was. "Although she's staying with Reagan's mom until my parents get there tomorrow, so we're a little worried about her."

"Mama does okay in short-term situations," Reagan admonished her husband. "Bri will be fine."

"I'm guessing your mother doesn't know about..." Jacob gestured to everything going on around them.

"No. We didn't see the point in needlessly worrying her. I'm sure we'll have Madison back by morning." Reagan's body language didn't match the assured tone of her words. She probably subscribed to that universe bullshit, too.

"Jacob, let's go to my office, and I can brief you on what we know," Dante said, and started walking toward his study, not bothering to check to see if Jacob was following.

Of course he was.

His phone began to vibrate in his pocket. He pulled it out and saw it was Tink. *Good, that means she made it to Houston okay.* As much as he wanted to talk to her, now wasn't the best time, and he silenced the call—sending it to voicemail.

"I hope you haven't spent that million dollars we paid you," was how Dante started.

"It wasn't the Colombians. It was Los Zetas—making it look like the Colombians did it. Think about it. Who would have the most to gain with you going to war in South America? Your resources would be spread thin; you'd be vulnerable, ripe for the picking if an attack from the West hit you while your manpower was in Colombia."

The Mexican stared at him as if trying to decipher whether he was purposefully trying to steer him wrong.

"The Zetas are here. I know it. Give me two days to prove it."

"You have thirty-six hours. Then we're going to war in Cartagena."

Dante was normally a reasonable man, but the man's daughter's life was on the line, so his irrationality made sense. As did his wife's proclamation to Jacob and Edward of, "I'm going with you."

"No, you're not," Edward and Dante said in unison, which seemed to only piss her off.

Her husband was astute enough to take another tack.

Drawing her into his arms, he murmured into her hair, "Bella, I need you here with me, *mi amor*. I'll go insane without you."

"Then come with us," she whispered.

He shook his head. "We need to be here, coordinating everything. I want to know what's going on with every single person who is looking for Madi and for the people who took her. We can't concentrate on just this one lead—that's what Edward and Jacob are for."

"Marcus, Eddie, Erik, and Raul just landed," Edward informed them as he looked at his phone. "We're meeting them in thirty minutes. We got this, Bella. Trust me."

Marcus was Edward's brother and former CIA. He was who they'd rescued in Cartagena two years ago, when Edward had kidnapped Reagan—before she was his wife, and drew Bella out of retirement to assist him. Eddie Landon, Erik Yu and Raul Garcia were three rebels from his brother's team who had disobeyed orders and come back to Colombia to get Marcus home safely. They, too, were coming out of retirement to assist.

Jacob wished he would have been a part of team like that. Marcus called them, and they came—no questions asked. Jake had always been a lone wolf—even when he was with the agency.

The only one of the four who knew Bella's true identity was Marcus, and that was only because his brother ended up married to Bella's sister. The other three were told as little as possible in Cartagena; they had been undercover long enough to respect they didn't need to know their assisting operative's bio. And Jacob had made damn sure their paths didn't cross, in the slim chance one of them recognized her somehow, some way.

He didn't know how he was going to keep her identity secret this time.

"I don't care—just get my daughter back!" was her response when he voiced his concerns out loud.

"I honestly think my brother's team will keep her secret. They know they're rescuing the daughter of the woman who played a pivotal part in Marcus's rescue. They've been around long enough to figure out the score."

Meaning they knew the CIA's termination orders of one of their own wasn't always justified—more like a convenient way to tie up loose ends. Edward was a prime example.

"I think they know when to let dead dogs lie," Jacob agreed.

"Everyone has a price," Dante observed cynically.

"So just be willing to beat it," Jacob responded.

"Whoever gets my little girl back can name their price."

Jacob and Edward started loading their gear bags with hi-tech goodies provided by the Sinaloa cartel while Bella stood watch. He knew old habits die hard, and she was itching to lead the charge with this.

"We got this. I promise you." Edward flung the duffle over his shoulder.

She looked at them both with pursed lips, then subtly nodded her head in agreement and stepped aside.

Edward grabbed Reagan and kissed the breath out of her, whispering words Jacob couldn't make out when they came up for air. She stroked his cheek and nodded with tears in her eyes.

Without another word, the two men got into separate vehicles and began communicating via walkie talkie, en route to pick up the rest of the ragtag gang of retired badasses.

Chapter Twenty-Nine

Taren

She heard the burner phone alert with a message around midnight, right when she was starting to doze off, and she bolted upright, fumbling to grab it from her dresser.

I'm glad you're home safe, baby. Things are going to be hectic here for a while, so not sure when or if I can call. I'll try to text soon.

I miss you. No word yet on Madi?

Miss you too, babe. No, not yet. We've got some good leads we're pursuing though.

Be careful. I love you. Hurry back to me.

I'll get there as soon as I can. xoxo

She breathed in the smell of the shirt she was holding against her chest like a security blanket. She might have 'accidentally' put one of his dirty shirts in her suitcase instead of his this morning when she packed his clothes. It had his natural scent, plus a mixture of the cologne and deodorant he wore.

As much as she missed him, she felt a sense of pride knowing that he was off saving the day. He needed to be in Ensenada.

Getting up so early this morning helped her fall back asleep, despite the two-hour time difference.

She showed up at 11:00 a.m. for her twelve hour shift in the ER, raring to go. As was often the case, she barely stopped the entire time she was on duty, and dragged herself home by a quarter to midnight, barely keeping her eyes open as she waited in her t-shirt and panties for her microwave dinner to cook.

She hadn't heard from Jacob yet today, but hoped to soon. It was after midnight when he texted last night, maybe it'd be like that tonight as well.

Turns out, he did, she was just dead asleep by ten after twelve and didn't hear the message alert.

Her 8:00 a.m. alarm had been going off for five minutes before it even registered with her.

This two-hour jet lag is kicking my ass, she thought when she finally got of bed an hour later. She'd fallen back asleep, then when she did wake up again, she saw Jake's text and composed a reply before throwing back the covers. Her pace around her apartment was slow-moving, and she felt like she was conserving her energy for when she went to work.

Taren repeated this cycle for the next two days until she was off for four. But even on the days she was home, she had a hard time getting motivated and spent most of her time reading or watching television. The following week was more of the same, although she picked up an additional shift to help out a co-worker, but then didn't even get out of her pajamas on her days off and ate mostly takeout.

I must be situationally depressed. The situation—or stressor, being Jacob's absence, of course, along with the uncertainty of what was happening with little Madison. Two weeks without a sign of her couldn't be good. She was ashamed to admit she was glad for the exhaustion when she came home at night—it let her sleep without thinking too much about it. When her brain wasn't shut down, she was filled with anxiety.

She talked to Jacob briefly about every other day, and he was as elusive as usual on the most recent call, although he hinted he might be home soon. But even that didn't perk her up.

Then the vomiting started after she ate breakfast the next morning, and again anytime she tried to eat anything.

Oh, fuck.

****

Jacob

The ransom request Dante had received still made it seem like the Colombians were behind Madison's abduction, so his respect for Jacob appeared to be at an all-time low. The Mexican didn't seem to have a lot of patience to listen to Jacob continue to insist Los Zetas were holding his daughter captive—although, he'd held off on going to war, for now. Jake decided it was best if Edward liaised with his brother-in-law on behalf of the small group from now on.

They'd pursued lead after lead like they were on a wild goose chase. Some were dead ends, some resulted in useful information, and they hadn't had to kill anyone yet—just bribe a few people. But Jacob knew how quickly that could change.

The latest information had them staking out a warehouse storing goods the street vendors sold that came in on cargo ships from China—a lot like in his dream. It was a little unnerving, but he also knew in his gut that meant she was there.

They didn't want to go in with guns blazing until they knew what they were dealing with. The risk of Madi getting killed outweighed everything else. So, they were developing a way to surreptitiously get a video feed into the building, assess the layout, and figure out whether or not she was even inside, and if so, where. If the opportunity arose, they'd go in like a hurricane, snatch her up and get her the hell out of there. Otherwise they'd devise a plan to extract her covertly. The problem was, unlike operatives who'd they'd gone in and rescued, the little girl had no idea they would be coming for her or even who they were, so there was always the chance she'd either hide from them or scream upon their arrival—if she were able to do either.

They were looking at aerial footage of the roof Eddie had taken earlier that morning. It would have been safer to do it by drone, but if a drone was heard and spotted, the Zetas—or Colombians—whoever it was really holding her, would know they'd been compromised. Jacob couldn't risk them getting spooked; he had no idea how they'd react. His 'Taren' phone—the phone he used only to communicate with her, dinged with an incoming message.

Jacob casually looked down and couldn't help but smile when he saw she'd sent him a picture. There's no way his Tinkerbell would have sent him nudes... was there? *God, that would be fucking awesome.* Although he seriously doubted she really had, he decided to wait until he was alone to open the attached photo.

As they went over the plan for breaching the roof to use a camera, his mind kept wandering back to the photo that was waiting for him to open on his phone. It was probably something benign, like a copy of her resignation letter.

But what if it wasn't?

Fuck, he missed holding her. Obviously—since he was getting all worked up about the slim possibility she'd sent him a picture of her naked boobs. Or maybe her body. *Oh, hell yes. Boobs, body, anything.* He'd suggested it in jest the last time they talked, more because he knew her reaction would make him laugh than anything, but also on the off-chance she'd comply.

"Yo, Smith," Erik said, snapping his fingers in front of Jake's face.

He shook his head. "Sorry, wandered off there for a second."

"Dude, we need your head in the game. Kinda got a little girl's life to save here," Eddie rebuked with a grin.

"I know. I'm sorry." He gestured with his hand. "Please, continue. I'm all ears."

All four men looked at him blank-faced. Finally, Edward spoke up.

"Um, we were kind of hoping you'd weigh in on this. None of us are familiar with the new camera you have."

"Oh, right. Yeah," he said then started to explain how the hi-tech gadget worked. When he finished the tutorial, he called for a five-minute break before they rehashed their plan one more time to flesh out any weak spots.

"You okay?" Edward asked as he fell in step with Jake as the older man made his way to the bathroom—where he'd be alone to look at Taren's picture.

"Yeah, just—"

"Worried about Taren," Edward supplied.

"A little."

"I get it. That's why I agreed to let Reagan come down here when she insisted on being with Bella, although part of me wishes she were home with Bri, but I know my parents are taking good care of her. You've got nobody watching over Taren."

"She checks in with me a few times a day, so I know she's doing all right, and we talk on the phone. I know she's really worried about Madi, and me."

"Not me?" Edward pouted.

"She's on a need-to-know basis; she has no idea you're with me."

"Probably a good idea."

"I wouldn't have even told her about Madi except she could tell something was really wrong the last night of our cruise, plus I had to explain why I wasn't returning with her."

"Returning to?"

"You're on a need-to-know basis, too." Jacob grinned. "And you don't need to know."

"I'll get it out of you," Edward said confidently, walking into the kitchenette area of the tiny apartment they'd holed up in.

"Don't bet on it," he said, escaping into the bathroom to finally get a look at the photo Taren sent.

Jacob was leaning against the vanity, grinning in anticipation when his jaw dropped as he looked at what appeared on his screen. He turned and stumbled backward and sank down onto the toilet, fully clothed, staring at the picture on his phone.

He scrubbed his jaw with the webbing of his hand, then used two fingers to blow up the image on the screen.

Two pink lines all right.

She'd simply sent him a picture of a home pregnancy test with the results visible.

He was going to be a dad.

Chapter Thirty

Jacob

Before he got his hopes up, he needed to call her and make sure he wasn't misunderstanding her text. It seemed pretty self-explanatory, but, he was a guy, after all. There was always a chance he was misconstruing something.

"Hello?" her sweet voice answered softly.

"Hey, Tink," he tried to say as quietly as he could. Even practically whispering, his words echoed off the walls in the tiny room.

"I'm guessing you got my picture."

"I did, baby. Does it mean what I think it means?"

"We're going to have a baby."

He combed his fingers through his hair, a million questions swirling through his mind, but thought he'd better start with the most important.

"How are you feeling? Are you okay?"

"I've just been tired and having a hard time keeping food down. That's why I thought to get a test."

"You're just barely pregnant; I thought you had to wait like a week after you missed your period before you could even take a test?" That's what he'd remembered anyway from the one time he and his high school girlfriend had a scare.

"Well, that would have been last week, but I didn't think much about the fact that I didn't get it. My periods are usually light anyway. I'm not really sure how this has happened, to be honest. I take my pills religiously. I'm kind of still in shock."

"Good shock, though, right?"

He could tell she was smiling when she said, "I'm getting used to the idea," but her voice quivered when she asked, "What about you? Are you okay with this news? I'm sorry to dump it on you like this when I don't even know if this was a good time for you, but I just took the test and…"

He cut her off, she was talking too fast and starting to babble.

"I'm over the moon, baby. You can text me anytime. If I'm in the middle of something I can't break away from"—*like directing a warehouse raid*—"I will call you back as soon as I can. If you have an emergency though, you need to text me with 911, and I will drop what I'm doing if I can."

"I'm sure everything will be fine. No emergencies."

"Promise me you'll text me if something happens."

"Jake, nothing is going to happen. Just hurry up and find Madi so you can come to Houston and be with me."

"I'll be there as soon as I can, beautiful."

He hung up, flushed the toilet for effect, washed his hands and walked into the living area. All four men were occupying the couch and chairs, grinning at him.

"What are you assholes looking at?" he snarled and kept walking into the kitchenette, opening the refrigerator and pretending to look for something other than the current contents of leftover takeout containers, water bottles, and beer.

Edward was the first to speak up. "So, Taren's pregnant? It's yours, right?"

Goddammit. He knew he hadn't been quiet enough. He kept his head in the fridge, trying to assess how he wanted to handle this and also trying to compose himself so he didn't rip Edward's head off for the question, *is it yours?*

Goddamn right that baby is mine.

The reality was sinking in.

Taren was carrying his baby.

They were going to be parents.

Holy shit. How was he going to keep her safe from fifteen hundred miles away?

Suddenly he felt a whole new wave of empathy for Dante and Bella. He'd known all of ten minutes that he was going to be a dad, and his baby was probably the size of a poppy seed, yet Jacob would already do whatever it took to protect him—or her. Always. He could only imagine how he was going to be when the baby finally arrived, or what he'd do if someone actually tried to take her—or him.

Did he want a boy or girl?

Fuck! Focus, man!

"Lose something in there?" Erik teased.

With a sigh, he grabbed a water bottle and closed the door, turning around to inquiring faces. They obviously weren't going to let it go.

"Yes, Taren is pregnant. No, we didn't plan it, but I'm excited as hell." He looked pointedly at Edward, "And don't ever fucking ask again if it's mine."

"Yeah, the second I said it, I realized it was kind of a dick question." The blond man grinned. "Congratulations, man. And welcome to the club."

****

Taren

She woke up late the next day; the guilt from sleeping so much subsided now that she understood why exactly she was feeling exhausted all the time. Managing to keep her breakfast of toast and juice down, she sat down at her computer to write her resignation letter. She gave the hospital a month's notice, thinking that was fair considering how accommodating they'd been with her recent last minute vacation request.

Taren thought about when the cruise tickets showed up—how skeptical she'd been that it wasn't a hoax, then when she found out they were real, allowing herself to be excited about it. It seemed like she'd been nothing but smiling ever since. She had been making baby steps before about being happy again in her life, but after reuniting with Jacob, it felt like those baby steps had turned into joyful leaps and bounds.

And now they were having a baby. A miracle baby, if you asked her. There's no way she should be pregnant.

No. Way.

Then a thought made her clutch her chest. What if her store-bought test gave her a false positive? She knew that happened. What if she wasn't really pregnant? What a cruel joke that would be, since she'd just allowed herself to feel excited about becoming a mother. And poor Jacob. He would be devastated.

She'd take a blood test tomorrow at work, just to be absolutely sure. But in her heart, Taren knew. Their baby was growing inside her—and she already loved him, or her, and would do anything to keep her little one safe.

****

Her Netflix binge came to an end right at ten o'clock, so she switched on the local news and walked into her closet to make sure she had clean scrubs for tomorrow.

The news anchor's voice as she walked back into her bedroom stopped her heart.

...The child's father had reportedly paid the ransom before authorities discovered her body in the Ensenada warehouse district. No arrests have been made.

Taren stood frozen, unable to process what she'd just heard. It wasn't possible. Madi couldn't be dead. Not that sweet little girl who'd held Jacob's hand and sat on his lap while they played dolls. No. It had to be a mistake.

She rewound the story from the beginning, tears streaming down her face as she listened and started to shake uncontrollably. When the anchor ended the story, she promptly ran to the bathroom and threw up, her head resting on the toilet as she sobbed.

She somehow ended up curled in a ball in her bed, the burner phone next to her as she waited to hear something—anything from Jacob. She'd sent him a text begging him to call her, but nothing yet.

What if... what if the same thing happened to her child? If someone could get to Madi with the armed guards surrounding the estate where she'd lived, what made Taren think someone wanting revenge on Jacob couldn't get to her baby? A sense of panic welled up inside her, and she had a sudden urge to hide in the closet. Her baby could be in real danger. Maybe Jacob had done the right thing in leaving her seven years ago. The moment those two pink lines had appeared, their entire future had changed. Dropping her hand to rub against her belly, she knew that from this point forward, she had to remember this was no longer just about her life. The safety of their baby was at stake.

Finally, a text from Jake.

Can't talk. I'll be in Houston by the morning. We'll talk then. I love you, Tink.

The day that had started out like a dream had quickly become a nightmare.

Chapter Thirty-One

Jacob

Reading Taren's text on the plane to Houston broke his heart.

Turned out to be a false positive. There's no baby.

I'm so sorry, Tinkerbell. Are you okay? I'm in the air, on my way to Houston now.

The sense of disappointment was overwhelming; he'd been so excited about becoming a dad; couldn't wait to see Taren's belly become round with his baby inside her, or have a little mini-Tinkerbell running around his place like Dante had a mini-Bella.

Watching the stoic Mexican come undone last night when they'd finally brought his baby home brought everyone watching to tears, including himself—although he'd been quick to brush them away and pretend like his eyes were itchy.

Jake needed to hold Taren again; he'd missed her so much these last few weeks, and he wasn't sure how she was handling the false positive news. Was she relieved? Or disappointed?

Maybe not having a baby right now was the best thing, after all. The mastermind behind Madi's kidnapping was still at large. Madi's disappearance had been hard enough on him—if it were his own child? He'd go insane.

I saw on the news about Madi. How are Bella and Dante holding up?

There wasn't a dry eye in the place.

He wasn't technically lying.

If Taren saw the news, then he knew their plan had been set in motion, and she thought Madi was dead. He needed to let her know the toddler was safe at John's house in San Diego. He could only imagine how upset she was.

The group—consisting only of her parents, godparents, and the five men who'd played a role in rescuing her, decided leaking Madison's 'death' was the best course of action at the moment. Dante wasn't convinced it was the Zetas who took his daughter, despite the tattoos on the men from the warehouse seeming to prove otherwise. And the survivors weren't talking—yet. Until the Sinaloans had absolute confirmation it was Los Zetas and not the Colombians, they weren't taking any chances. Letting the world believe Madi was dead was the best option in keeping her safe. Jacob wasn't going to risk telling Taren over the phone or via text that the little girl was alive and well, in case his phone had become compromised. The small group who knew she was returned home unharmed had taken an oath to only reveal it to those who absolutely needed to know—and *never* electronically. Jacob wouldn't be the weakest link in that chain with something as avoidable as using a compromised phone.

See you soon, baby.

Please don't come. I have some things I need to figure out.

Oh, no. That wasn't going to work.

We need to talk, Tink.

Please, Jake. Just let me go. I'm not cut out for this.

He considered honoring her request for all of point zero two seconds. He knew she had to be upset about Madison, but she just needed to hear him out.

Baby, let me explain some things.

When she didn't text back, he sent another.

Tinkerbell. I'll be on the ground in ninety minutes. It's going to be okay, baby. I promise.

Still, she didn't respond.

****

Taren

She called in sick to work, still devastated over the news of Madison. But Jacob's text of '*See you soon,*' sent her into a panicked frenzy. She needed to leave before he got to her apartment.

Now, she just needed to figure out a place to go. Of her old friends in town, they'd either slept with her ex-husband or faded out of her life because they thought her ex was an asshole.

Taren blew out a deep breath. That left her parents or her Aunt Rachel, and of the two, only her aunt was in Houston. Rachel was her dad's youngest sister; there was a sixteen-year difference between the two. Her grandparents had five children—her father was the oldest and Rachel was the youngest, which made her only ten years older than Taren.

"Of course you're welcome, honey," Rachel had said when she'd called and told her the *Reader's Digest* version of her sob story.

She threw a week's worth of clothes along with some toiletries into a suitcase and was out the door. Her aunt had hot tea and cookies waiting for her when she arrived, because 'hot tea and sugar make everything better'.

Rachel was a beautiful woman, if not a little eccentric, but also one of the kindest Taren had ever met. She'd gone through a divorce after a brief marriage in her early twenties and hadn't remarried or had children yet.

"I'm still waiting on the universe to bring my Mr. Right to me," she'd said at Christmas a few years back. "In the meantime, Mr. Right Now will have to do."

As Taren's favorite aunt growing up, Rachel had a big influence on her. Her dad described his youngest sister as a hippie chick. It wasn't meant to be disparaging, and Rachel certainly never took it that way. Some of her woo-woo beliefs, as Jacob calls them, rubbed off on her.

"You want to talk about it, sweets?" her aunt had asked once she settled in with her tea and cookies.

"Eventually, but not right now, if that's okay?"

"That's perfectly fine. *Mi casa es su casa.*"

"Thanks. I promise I won't be in your hair long, maybe just a week or so." *When I'm sure the coast is clear, and I can go back to my apartment.*

"Sweet girl, I'm happy to have you here. Stay as long as you want. Hell, I'd love to have a little one running around here."

"Yeah? How come you don't then?"

Rachel sighed and gave a sad smile. "It's not something I'm interested in doing alone and since Mr. Right seems to have gotten lost... I guess I always thought I'd have more time. Then, bam! I turned forty this year and am thinking maybe it's not meant to be."

"You never know; he might show up when you least expect it. Have you asked the universe to bring him to you?"

"You know what, I haven't explicitly asked. Maybe I should. But who's to say... maybe he won't want kids."

"Or maybe he already has ones who need a mother."

"Stranger things have happened," the beautiful blonde woman with pink streaks in her hair said with a smile.

"Universe, bring Rachel her Mr. Right and her family."

Her aunt laid her hands on Taren's belly and said with a soft smile. "Universe, help Taren figure out what to do next."

Taren knew it was going to be a long road ahead, but felt in her heart just then that everything would be okay. She'd have her happiness. Maybe it wouldn't be with Jacob, but perhaps this baby was what she was supposed to get from him. He or she would be her joy, so she wouldn't look at their brief reunion as anything but a blessing.

"I have my first doctor's appointment tomorrow; wanna come with me to my appointment?"

"You bet your heart-shaped butt I do! What time?"

Chapter Thirty-Two

She was curled up on the bed in Rachel's guest room reading her Kindle when her phone started dinging. She'd half been expecting this—Jacob must be in Houston.

At first, she decided she was just going to delete his messages without reading them, but her curiosity got the better of her. She was a glutton for punishment.

11:01 a.m. Tinkerbell, where are you. We need to talk. I need to explain some things, baby.

11:11 a.m. Just tell me where you are. I'll come to you.

11:22 a.m. Tink, please, baby. Everything isn't what you think.

11:36 a.m. Please, Taren. At least let me know you're okay. You owe me that much.

He was right. She did owe him that much—considering everything he'd probably been through with Madison, she was sure he was worried about her, too.

11:37 a.m. I'm okay. Please, just let me go.

It wasn't until she fired off the text that she realized she'd probably played right into his hand. She wouldn't be surprised if he was already in the process of tracing her message, and any minute now, he'd know her exact location—right down to where she was sitting in Rachel's house, and come pounding on her window.

Dammit! She quickly shut her phone off, not sure if that would make a difference or not, but it couldn't hurt.

****

Jacob

Oh, sweet Tinkerbell.

He wasn't sure why she'd shut her phone off suddenly. Maybe so she wouldn't read any more of his texts, but he somehow doubted it. If she'd gone to the trouble of disappearing from her apartment, she probably realized he would track her phone.

Unfortunately for her, he knew where she was the minute he walked away from her apartment door after banging on it until a neighbor came out and yelled at him; shutting off her phone wasn't going to change a thing. He had called up the app to find her phone before he even got back in his car and called his P.I. And just to be double sure, he clicked on the tracker that he'd forgotten to take out of her purse from the cruise.

Both came up to an address belonging to a Rachel Fairchild—a relative of hers, he assumed, judging by the last name.

The question that he now had to ponder—at least for the next day or so, was what he was going to do with that information. He'd left the airport half-cocked, but had since calmed down. He needed to play his cards right if he was going to get her to see him.

His bank had also notified him of a deposit made into his account. What Dante paid him for finding his little girl was enough to set him up for the rest of his life, had he not already been set. The ragtag team hadn't even given him a price for the job—Erik and Raul had stayed behind without asking for a dime. Jacob would have done it for free, and he was sure the other men felt the same, so apparently Dante set one for them. And it wasn't like they were going to send Dante's money back to him after he paid it.

Besides, Dante would not want to feel indebted to them any more than he already did. The astronomical sum the Mexican paid was his way of trying to even the score. Jacob respected that, because he was much the same way. While owing favors to people was a way of life in this business, he never wanted the scales tipped too far in someone else's favor. That's when they started thinking they owned him, and that shit didn't fly with men in Jacob and Dante's world.

Chapter Thirty-Three

"Congratulations, Mama... everything appears to be great. Looks like your due date is March twenty-fourth," Dr. Bonet said as she moved the wand slightly along her stomach that now had goo all over it.

It was such a bittersweet moment. She was smiling brightly at Rachel, because she really was happy, but inside her heart was hurting because Jacob wasn't here with her. He would have been over the moon.

"Any ideas for a name?" her aunt asked after the doctor left the room, leaving Taren to wipe the mess off her stomach before getting dressed.

"No. Not yet. I'm going to wait until I know the sex before I really start thinking about that.

"I've always been partial to names of places, like Austin or Dakota."

Rachel kept talking the entire drive back to her place. Taren suspected she was trying to keep her from thinking too much. Her suspicions were confirmed, when they pulled into her aunt's driveway, and Rachel grabbed her hand before getting out.

"It's going to be okay. You're smart, and you're young, and you come from a long line of strong women. Not to mention you have a support system of badasses. The universe has your back, sweets. I promise."

"I know," Taren said with a genuine smile. "I think I just need a little time to grieve."

"Take all the time you need."

"Thank you. For everything. For letting me stay, and going with me today. I really appreciate it. And for not pressuring me to talk about it."

"You'll talk about it when you're ready. Or not. Either way, I'm here for you."

"I know. I love you for that. And I'm always here for you, too."

Rachel leaned over and kissed her niece on the cheek. "Have a good day at work. Maybe you should talk to them about reducing your hours."

She shook her head. "No. I need all the money I can get.

Rachel cocked her head. "You aren't going to ask for child support?"

"That would mean telling him about the baby..."

"And you don't want to do that?"

"No," Taren said softly, looking down at her lap.

"You don't owe me an explanation, sweets," her aunt said, opening the car door. "I trust you have your reasons. I'm here for you."

Taren mouthed, *Thank you* with a meek smile before putting the car in reverse. She was humbled by her aunt's support.

It's going to be a good day, she thought as she put the Kia in drive. Still, she couldn't shake the feeling that Jake was going to show up at the hospital, and she was going to fall apart the second she saw him. She kept her phone shut off, just in case he really could track her.

She got through her shift without Jacob appearing and crawled into bed in her most comfortable pajamas. Maybe he was going to honor her wishes after all.

Why did a tiny bit of her heart feel disappointed about that?

She put a hand on her stomach *It's for the best.*

That tiny bit of her heart that was feeling disappointed about him leaving her alone whispered, "*Is it though?*"

"Yes, it is!" she said out loud before punching her pillow and rolling onto her side. Thankfully, sleep came quickly, thanks in part to working a twelve-hour day.

Saturday morning Rachel suggested they go out for breakfast then do some retail therapy afterward.

"Let's at least look at some baby things afterward. You don't have to buy anything yet, but it will be fun to look."

That actually sounded fun.

Sitting across from her in the little breakfast diner, Rachel's face turned somber.

"You need to let your parents know about the baby, sweets. Your mother would wring my neck if she found out I knew about her future grandchild and she didn't. And I'm sure as hell not facing the wrath of your father. You need to call them."

Taren compromised and, after fishing her phone out of her purse, texted them instead. There were no new messages when she turned it on.

That was a good thing, she reminded herself. He was honoring her wishes. She wasn't disappointed at the empty mailbox. Not. At. All.

The text was pointless in avoiding talking to her mother because her phone started ringing almost immediately after sending it. She looked down at the screen and scowled at a grinning Rachel across the booth.

"Don't you dare send your mother to voicemail," her aunt chided.

She tried to be quiet in the slow restaurant when she answered. Her mother was over the moon, and she had to hold the phone away from her ear at first.

"My first grandchild! Oh, Taren. This is so exciting."

"Thanks, Mom. I'm pretty excited, too."

"Who's the father? It's not David's is it, honey?"

"No. Remember Jacob? The guy I dated in college? We kind of had a little fling—he was the one who bought my cruise."

"Of course I remember Jacob. You were head over heels in love with him. He was the one who bought your trip? Oh, that is so romantic. You two ended up together in the end, after all. And to top it off, you're going to have a baby! Things have a way of working themselves out, don't they, honey?"

She didn't have the heart to tell her they weren't together, or that Jake didn't even know about their child. Maybe she didn't want to say the words out loud.

"Yeah, they do, Mom."

"How are you feeling? Are you having morning sickness? I was terribly sick the first three months of my pregnancy with you, then it miraculously went away."

"It's hit or miss most days."

"When are you due?"

"March twenty-fourth."

Her mom was silent for a moment, and Taren knew she was doing some quick calculations in her head.

"You're just barely pregnant! Have you been to the doctor?"

"I went to the doctor yesterday. I had my first ultrasound and everything looked fine."

Across the booth, Rachel was making a slashing motion across her neck and mouthing, "Don't tell her I was with you."

It was Taren's turn to grin. She had no intention of telling her mom because it would hurt her feelings, but it was fun to make her beautiful aunt sweat a little.

"Have you talked to Aunt Rachel lately?"

****

Monday morning, she was on her laptop paying bills and answering emails, when she received an email alert about a deposit to her bank. As she clicked open the website, she wondered if something had happened that delayed her paycheck, even though she'd received that email on Friday.

Her totals came up, and she knew there hadn't been a delay with the hospital's payment to her. Her checking account had one hundred and twenty-five thousand more than it should.

The line item read *Misc—for baby*.

Her world started spinning. How did he know? It wasn't possible.

Yet, there it was in black and white on her bank statement. No one else had that kind of money to just put in her checking account for *miscellaneous* items.

Then, she went to her car Tuesday evening after work and found a dozen roses in her front seat along with a mint green baby's onesie with white lettering that read *I get my charm from my daddy*.

The only reason she turned on her phone was to see if Rachel had texted her about needing her to pick anything up on her way home. *The only reason.*

It wasn't to see if there were any incoming texts from him.

Saturday: Baby, please talk to me. There's some things I need to tell you, and some things you need to tell me, too, apparently.

Saturday: Tinkerbell, let me take you out to dinner. Please?

Sunday: Good morning, beautiful. I miss waking up next to you. Can we get breakfast and talk?

Monday: I deposited some money into your account. Please, just accept it. I have an obligation to our child, too.

Monday: Dinner tonight?

Nothing so far on Tuesday. Maybe he was trying a new approach, since she hadn't replied to his texts, by breaking into her car and leaving her flowers and a baby present.

"Doesn't matter," she said out loud as she started her car. "It's not going to work. He should understand better than anyone why we can't be together."

She waited until she was on the road before telling her hands-free app to, "Call Rachel."

"Okay, calling Jacob."

"No!" she yelled and quickly ended the call.

Rachel was going to get a kick out of this.

She tried again.

"Call Ray—chelll."

"Okay, calling Jacob."

Again, she disconnected the call as soon as she could.

She shook her head and smiled in spite of herself. *That son of a bitch hacked my hands-free app.* What else had he done?

Just then her phone started ringing. Of course it was him; she'd called him twice—or, at least her phone had.

Taren answered with, "Did you hack my phone?"

"Did I hack your phone?" came the deep voice that she'd missed.

"That was my question."

"Well, technically, no. *I* did not hack your phone."

"Jake, you can't just pay someone to get what you want. What part of *do not contact me* did you not understand?"

"The part before where I said I need to talk to you—in person. There are things I can't talk about on the phone, Tink."

"There's nothing to say. Being with you isn't safe for our child, Jake. If people could get to Madison and murder her, you don't think they could get to our baby? I'm not risking it."

He sighed. "I don't want to talk about this over the phone, Taren. And, I don't want you talking about me over the phone with anyone, either. That's why I need to see you in person."

So that explained how he knew. He must have been having her followed and the P.I. overheard her conversation with her mom in the restaurant.

"I have to go. Unfuck my hands-free so I don't get in a wreck having to dial people I actually want to talk to."

With that, she disconnected the call. And promptly started crying—the unfairness of it all overwhelming her. The tears were flowing so hard and fast that she had to pull over into a parking lot until she was finished.

Stupid pregnancy hormones.

****

Jacob

She'd fucking lied to him.

It wasn't a false fucking positive. She was pregnant.

When the initial shock wore off over what his private investigator told him he'd heard in the booth next to hers in the diner Saturday morning, he made some phone calls. Yeah, he might have had her medical records hacked for confirmation, but he'd never admit that.

All the feelings he'd felt that day in the bathroom in Ensenada when he'd looked at the picture with the two pink lines came flooding back to him. The excitement, the fear, the protectiveness, the wonder...

They were having a baby.

Her disappearing act made more sense now.

He kind of adored her mama bear instincts. She was, after all, protecting *his* cub. It actually made him love his little sprite even more.

But she needed to know that no one would protect their baby better than he would. He just needed to talk to her and convince her of that.

He might need to call in reinforcements.

****

"Jacob Smith. Were your ears burning?"

Bella's pretty face appeared on the video screen, and he grinned back at her.

"No. Should they be?"

"Ortiz has been asking about you."

Ortiz was the code name they'd agreed upon for Madison. He had no idea why or how they came up with it, and he didn't ask. Wendy was Taren's code name, after Wendy in *Peter Pan.*

"Maybe if you help me out with Wendy, we could come visit you."

Jacob then told her about the baby.

"Holy shit! Congratulations! You were together, what, ten days? You've got some strong swimmers." Bella grinned.

"Except I haven't seen her since I arrived after leaving Ensenada after Madi died. So..."

"So she thinks her baby isn't safe."

He shook his head.

"Fuck, that's not good, Jacob."

"No, it's not, and she won't take my calls so I can explain. She thinks she's hiding out from me at her aunt's—which she's obviously not. So, I either show up at her work or show up unannounced at her aunt's. Either way, I'm going to come off as a stalker, and she's going to shut down before hearing me out."

"So, I'm guessing this is the part where I come in?"

"If you'll help me."

"Are you kidding right now? Of course I'll help you. Not only am I indebted to you for, like, the rest of my life, but I freaking want to help because, who doesn't love a good love story?"

He sighed. "It's not a good love story yet."

"Oh, it will be, let me handle it."

"What are you going to do?"

"Ambush her—Jones sister style. Just let me run it by Dante, and I'll be on a plane in the morning."

"Thanks, Bella. I really appreciate it."

"Name your baby after me if it's a girl, and we'll call it even."

Chuckling, he agreed. "If I have any say with this baby, consider it done."

They were quiet for a moment, his smile fading into a sigh. "If she'd just listen to me... I could clear this up in thirty seconds."

"We'll get this fixed. I promise."

His laugh was humorless. "How can you be so sure?"

"To quote Westley, from *The Princess Bride*, '*This is true love; you think this happens every day?*' You two are meant to be together. No way is a little misunderstanding going to come between you two."

"I feel so fucking helpless. Like, if I could just get her to talk to me—"

"That's where I come in. I know it's hard, but try to be patient. And don't do anything to make this worse."

"No promises."

"Don't make me hurt you. Because not only am I capable—I will."

"Thanks again."

"See you tomorrow."

He blew out a long breath when he hung up. *I can be patient.* He'd waited seven years for her—he could get through another day. But, she had to be scared and feeling alone, and that really bothered him. He could only imagine how much she was hurting, thinking Madison had been murdered and worried about their child's safety.

Don't worry, baby. I'll be there to protect you soon.

He already had round-the-clock surveillance on her, but nothing could replace him being there to take care of her.

The Jones sisters couldn't get here soon enough.

Chapter Thirty-Four

Taren

She opened the door to one of the triage rooms and almost fainted. There on the side of the hospital bed kicking her little feet back and forth was Madison Guzman while her mother, Bella sat in a chair next to her and her Aunt Reagan sat in a chair by the wall.

"Madi?" Taren gasped before tears started streaming down her face.

"Hi, Miss Taren," the little girl said with a smile right before Taren grabbed both her hands in order to feel that she was really there and not some hallucination she was having.

"Hello, *mamacita*," Bella said with a polite smile. "This is what Jacob has been trying to talk to you about." Bella's tone sounded a lot like her mom's when she was trying to refrain from scolding her. "He couldn't tell you about this electronically. I'm sure you can understand why."

"So you came all the way from California?"

"Well, technically, I came from South Dakota," Reagan piped in.

"I can't believe this," she said, stroking the little girl's downy hair. "I was so heartbroken for you all."

"It was definitely a harrowing time."

Reagan stood and helped the little girl off the table. "Let's grab a drink from the vending machine, little miss."

"How is she doing?" Taren asked, looking in the direction Reagan and Madi had just disappeared.

"She's okay. We've had a counselor out twice to do play therapy with her, and she seems to have settled back into a routine. Dante and I are still wrecks though, and it's been a struggle not to camp out in her bedroom every night and make sure she's safe. Of course my husband has put in cameras with night vision with a state of the art security system in our new house in California."

"I'm getting a new dog!" Madi proclaimed loudly when she walked back in.

"You are? What kind of dog?"

She glanced at Bella, who had just picked her daughter up in her arms.

"The local PetSmart has rescue groups come and do adoptions every weekend. We're going to go next weekend and see if we can find our next family member."

"Have you decided on a name yet?"

"Uh huh," the little girl nodded solemnly.

"What is it?"

"Jacob!" she said, erupting into a fit of giggles.

Taren couldn't help but smile.

"Ever since he found her, he's all she talks about."

Taren interrupted. "Jake was the one who rescued Madi?"

Bella's smile was wistful as she stroked her daughter's hair "He did. He was relentless; God love him. He never gave up. None of the six did. I owe my daughter's life to him."

"And that's why you're here."

"No!" she exclaimed as she moved Madi to her other hip. "Okay, yes, maybe. He's one of the good guys, Taren. I've known Jacob for a lot of years, and not once he has not been true to his word."

Taren huffed out a laugh. "He continually lied to me for the first three years that I knew him."

Bella tsked at her as she set Madi down, and once again, Reagan disappeared with her.

"You can't hold the fact he didn't tell you he worked for the government against him. That is something that is drilled into an agent—it was part of his training, and frankly, it's a mandatory directive."

She shrugged. "I guess. He said the same thing."

The former agent's face softened. "He saved my little girl, Taren. He'd never let anything happen to your child. I just wish you'd at least hear what he has to say. Then you can make your decision. But I'd hate for you to have regrets ten years from now because you didn't at least hear his side of things—especially when you're having a child together. Wouldn't it be better to air things out now?"

"But his job," Taren said softly.

"You think he gives a damn about his job?"

"He gave a damn enough about it to leave me seven years ago."

"No. He gave a damn enough about *you* to leave you seven years ago. Do you really believe if he honestly thought he couldn't keep you safe now—especially carrying his baby—that he wouldn't just let you go?"

"You're probably right."

"Of course I'm right. I'm always right. Now, go get the next couple of days off. We're going on a girls' trip. Don't argue with me."

"I need to talk to Jake."

Reagan reappeared and patted her back as they walked out of the room. "Don't worry, honey. Wherever you are, I guarantee Jacob isn't far behind. He'll find you."

Chapter Thirty-Five

Taren

Luckily she'd changed her shifts to only eight hours a day and had been able to take a half day off, saying she wasn't feeling well. Which would lend credence when she called in sick tomorrow.

Reagan and Bella were already waiting for her at Rachel's house with a bottle of champagne and a bottle of sparkling cider for her. Madison was safely with Reagan's in-laws, who were also taking care of Brianna for the few days they were going to be gone.

Her aunt came into the living room with two suitcases.

"We're all set," she said with a smirk.

"Yes! Let's get this show on the road!" Reagan declared as she raised her glass.

"Wait. Where exactly are we going?"

"Mexico," Bella said nonchalantly as she tried to usher her toward to the door. "Your mom and aunts are meeting us there."

She stood in the entryway, frozen in confusion.

"We're going to Mexico? Right now? And my family is meeting us there? Why?"

Bella looped her arm through Taren's right arm, while Reagan looped her arm through Taren's left, and the two sisters escorted her out the door as Rachel locked up behind them.

"Yes, *mamacita*. We're going to have a baby shower for you in Mexico. It's going to be two days of fun in the sun, and you're going to have to a great time surrounded by people who love you—whether you want to or not.

She smiled and took the glass of sparkling cider Bella offered her as they piled in the waiting car for the short ride to the airport.

"We'll have lunch on the plane," Bella announced.

"I've never ridden on a private jet before," Rachel exclaimed with excitement.

"Taren has," Bella said, looking at her slyly. "Her baby daddy has one."

Rachel's eyes got wide. "Oh really?"

"I never rode on his plane," was her only response.

Jake. She needed to talk to him in person. She hoped Reagan was right, and he wasn't far behind.

Their time on the jet passed quickly and before she knew it, they had arrived at the Guzman estate. Security continued to remain tight, with the guards scrutinizing the women and checking the car before allowing them through the gates. Taren assumed that meant they hadn't caught whoever had orchestrated Madison's kidnapping, but decided it wasn't an appropriate time to ask.

In addition to her mother and aunts already being there, a stunning dark-haired woman named Quinn joined them. She seemed to work for Bella's company and, judging by all the teasing she was getting, was maybe dating John—

Madison's godfather, who also appeared to be the woman's boss.

Apparently, there was also a whole gaggle of men—her father and uncles included, golfing with Dante, John, and Edward and staying nearby. They were joining the ladies in the morning for a day of planned activities. There was no mention of Jake being with them, and she was afraid to ask if he was there.

Maria and Rosa sat down briefly and presented her with gifts, although they seemed happiest when they were serving food rather than sitting and eating it, and disappeared to the kitchen once she'd opened their beautiful, thoughtful presents—a handmade, crocheted blanket and a delicate lace baptismal gown.

The women were served an elegant dinner and made their way onto the patio afterward. It wasn't long before they decided to take advantage of the pool and hot tub, and quickly disappeared to change into their suits.

Taren had opened a ridiculous amount of gifts earlier, then they had played some silly games while laughing and drinking. Well, everyone but Taren drank—she stuck with sparkling cider. It had been a really fun day, but she was getting tired—especially once the sun went down. The time difference catching up to her.

"I think I'm going to turn in," she told Bella with a smile. "Thank you so much for today. I really needed it. I can't believe how generous you've been."

"It was my pleasure." The redhead smiled, then paused, her face turning somber. "Have you talked to Jacob?"

"No, why? Is he here?"

Bella gave a sly smile. "That's the rumor."

"Here? Like, here-here?"

"No, not at the estate. But in Ensenada. A little birdy told me his plane landed about an hour ago. I'd be willing to bet money he'll be at breakfast."

Taren fought back a smile.

"Well, goodnight, then. I'll see you in the morning."

"Bright and early, I'm sure," Bella teased before heading back to the patio.

Chapter Thirty-Six

Jacob

He was staying at a nearby villa in Ensenada. The same one Edward and Reagan had stayed in when Edward was recovering from being shot in Cartagena. The rest of the men were also staying in the same gated complex, only in smaller casitas. Jake thought Edward and Dante would more than likely return to their wives tonight at the estate.

If all went according to plan, he'd be spending tomorrow night here with Tinkerbell before flying her to Bora Bora for their honeymoon on Sunday.

He'd paid for her parents and aunts and uncle to fly in, under the guise that it was her baby shower, and the men were tagging along for some golf and sightseeing. He knew it was a risk, but his family was also arriving tomorrow.

Once he got her to listen and agree to trust him to keep their baby safe, he wasn't taking any chances—he was marrying her tomorrow night come hell or high water. He'd even enlisted Bella and Reagan's help buying her a dress and planning the ceremony.

"What if she doesn't want to be with you?" Bella bluntly asked.

"She has to. Because I can't fucking live without her."

Their time apart had been nothing short of hell for him. Worse than when he'd broken up with her seven years ago— and that had felt like his heart had been ripped out of his chest. But this was ten times worse because he had so much more to lose.

His phone dinged with a text from Bella.

I think if you came for breakfast tomorrow, you wouldn't be thrown out. LOL

Can I come right now?

Probably not a good idea—she just went to bed.

Not the answer he wanted but he didn't feel he needed to say so. *Okay. See you in the morning.*

Still, he decided to at least try to engage Taren tonight. If nothing else, so she'd know he was thinking of her.

He fired off a brief text.

Hope you're enjoying your time with everyone in Mexico.

To his surprise, the little dots indicating she was replying showed up right away.

I am. Everyone is having a blast. Bella and Dante have been incredibly generous. Yet...

Yet?

Yet, I can't help but wish you were here.

What if I were?

The dots started and stopped several times, like she was writing a text, then deleting it. Finally:

I would be glad.

That was all he fucking needed to be out the front door and in his rented sedan. At this time of night, he was at the estate in eight minutes, and through security, walking up the front steps in five. He could hear a party in the backyard—maybe he could slip in a back door so he wouldn't have to ring the doorbell and announce his presence. He really didn't need a lecture from Bella tonight.

Jacob knew which room she was staying in—all he needed to do was get inside undetected.

He'd kept her texting on the drive over. Luckily, the streets were deserted so there was no one to honk at him if he took too long at the red light tapping out his reply. And he'd continued once he'd gotten inside the house.

Yeah?

Seeing Bella today in the ER today with her companions... that blew me away. And she said some things that made sense.

Like what?

That I should hear you out.

Nodding, his fingers flew to agree. *Bella is a wise woman. You should listen to her.*

Maybe we can talk sometime soon.

Why not now?

He waited until he heard the ding on the other side of the door before knocking softly.

That's you at my bedroom door, isn't it?

It is.

What if I'm not ready to talk?

Then I'll leave.

Jake, it's late.

He leaned his forehead against the mahogany door and closed his eyes. She was so close... Yet, he knew better than to push her too hard. She was just starting to respond to him; he didn't want her pulling away because he came on too strong.

His fingers were far slower tapping out his response. *Okay. Maybe tomorrow?*

But whispered out loud, "Please, Tinkerbell."

She must have padded to the door without him hearing because, clearly, she was just on the other side of it when he uttered the words and immediately opened the door.

Standing before him in a white cotton with red cherries pajama set, she looked fragile, and he clenched his fist, feeling his nails dig into his palms as he kept himself from reaching out to her. Her eyes were filled with a sadness he'd only seen in the photographs from when her marriage to David was imploding. The skin peeking out from under her shirt almost killed him. That was *his* baby in her belly, and he couldn't fucking hold her, or talk to her stomach like he'd been dreaming of doing.

"Hi, Tink."

She offered a polite smile. "Hi."

"May I come in?"

With a small sigh, like it was against her better judgment, she moved to the side so he could pass through the doorway, then closed it behind him—her arms immediately wrapping around her body as she walked toward the sitting area.

Once she was seated on the couch, he tried to start talking, only to realize he didn't even know where to begin. As if on instinct, he dropped to his knees in front of her and reached for her hand—staring her in the eye as he pledged, "I love you, Tinkerbell. And that little pumpkin seed you're growing inside of you."

"But—"

"No, buts, baby. We need to be a family."

"What if something happens, like Madi?"

"Madi's safe."

"But she wouldn't have been if..." Tears started streaming down her face. "If you hadn't saved her."

He stroked her arm cautiously. "I'd never let anything happen to you or our child. You have my word."

"I don't know, Jake. If you're still traveling for work, we'll be alone."

"I'll quit."

She started laughing even as she kept crying.

"I'm guessing you can't just quit."

He shrugged. "I'll bring a partner on and phase out."

The corner of her mouth turned up.

"You really do have an answer for everything, don't you?"

Jake winked. "It's why they pay me the big bucks."

They could hear laughter and yelling from the balcony, and she stood to close the door. Apparently she wasn't expecting him to follow her, because she turned around and ran straight into his chest. His arms came around her instinctively.

The pulse in her neck started to flutter, and a small blush crept up her chest and neck, while neither of them moved.

Finally, he motioned with his head toward the pool area where the noise was coming from.

"Why aren't you out there?"

"I was tired. Besides, I have no desire to be in a bathing suit right now. I feel puffy."

He smirked. "You don't look puffy." Then he ran his hands along her waist over her pajamas, relishing how she felt. "You don't feel puffy."

"Trust me, I'm puffy."

"You might have to prove that to me."

She stared at him for a beat before muttering, "How?"

Boldly, he started unbuttoning her cotton top. Taking his time, he savored the feel of her warm body as his fingers grazed her skin, all the while maintaining eye contact with her. Finally unfastening the last button, he pulled her shirt open and glanced down, smiling softly when he saw her skin pebbled in goosebumps.

She was so fucking beautiful. Her soft stomach as his baby grew inside her, her breasts visibly heavier than they were just a few weeks ago, and her nipples standing at attention once he pulled the fabric from her skin.

"Not puffy," he whispered, as he traced the backs of his fingertips along the outline of her tits. It was her move—would she pull away?

His gaze left her delicious tits and sought her eyes.

"I love you. You are my fucking world—I'll do whatever it takes to keep you."

Tears brimmed in her eyes and threatened to spill onto her cheeks, but she still hadn't pulled away from his touch. Emboldened, he slowly began to move his index finger past her cleavage and down her stomach, stopping just at the waistband of her pajama shorts.

She didn't flinch while returning his gaze. Cautiously, Jacob dipped his head until his mouth found hers. Warmth spread from his stomach to the rest of his body as the sensation of her lips on his filled him, and he deepened the kiss—unleashing the pent up fear that he'd never have the opportunity to do this again.

Her arms went around his neck while her fingers dug frantically into his hair, holding him close.

He held her back with one hand as his entire other hand splayed over her boob and began kneading her creamy flesh in his palm.

Dragging his lips against hers, he murmured, "I've missed you so much. God, baby, I've been dying inside without you."

"I've missed you, too," she panted back. Her fingertips skimmed the hem of his shirt until she gripped it and tugged it over his head.

Their bare flesh met, and he pulled her tighter to him while running one hand through her hair then tugging, his lips dragging across her exposed neck as he muttered, "You're never allowed to leave me again—do you understand?"

Her hands clawed at his back while she tilted her head and gasped, "I don't ever want to leave you again."

He stopped kissing her neck and stood up straight, his expression sober as he looked down at her.

"I will keep you safe, Tink." He put his hand on her stomach. "And him. Or her."

"Do you want a boy?"

"I just want my fucking family."

A tear rolled down her cheek, then another. He caught them with his fingertip.

"Don't cry."

"I was so scared, Jake."

"I know. I'm sorry. I'm sorry I wasn't there when you thought Madi was killed. I hope Bella explained why I couldn't tell you over the phone—and you were gone when I got to your apartment to explain. Then I found out you were lying about the baby, and I was beside myself. I needed to hold you. Protect you. Keep you safe." He slid her shirt off her, letting it drop to the floor, murmuring, "I'm never letting you go."

With that, he scooped her up into his arms and carried her to the bed that she'd already turned down, depositing her carefully before going back and shutting the light off. She switched the bedside lamp on and watched with a shy smile as he approached the four poster bed.

"You have quite the punishment coming, baby. But not tonight. Tonight, I need to love you all night long."

"I love the sound of that."

He tugged his pants off and lie next to her, still clad in his grey boxer briefs while she wore only her cotton shorts. When their bare chests met, he closed his eyes and whispered, "Never letting you go," then tugged her closer to him as if to emphasize the point.

"Good," she said as her lips caressed his neck. "I love you, Jacob Preston Smith."

"I love you, too, Taren Scarlett Fairchild-Smith."

He felt her giggle. "That's not my name."

"Just trying it on for size."

He'd talk to her later about getting married tomorrow. Right now, he needed to worship her body.

****

Taren

Words couldn't begin to describe how happy she felt as she nestled closer to Jacob in the early morning hours. He'd been true to his word and had loved her, literally, all night long. There were periods of rest, recovery, and pillow talk between rounds, but they didn't go to sleep until four in the morning, both exhausted. She fell asleep on top of him with a smile on her face, while he was still inside her.

Jacob's phone started ringing at nine thirty, and his voice was soft when he answered it.

"Hey, Bella."

Chuckling, he said, "How did you know?"

Taren nudged him and mouthed, *put it on speaker*.

"Because there are cameras throughout my house," came her hostess's scolding voice.

They both looked up at the ceiling for cameras. "Did you watch us—"

Bella started laughing. "Not in your room. But in the hallway outside your room. So, unless you went out the window last night—I knew you were still here. Not to mention, your car is still in the driveway."

"Good morning, Bella," Taren said softly.

"Good morning. Everyone has already had breakfast, and I sent Reagan and Edward to take them sightseeing so you two lovebirds could take your time getting around this morning. I wasn't sure how late you stayed up last night."

"Pretty late," Taren confessed, smiling at Jake as she did.

"It sounds like you two worked things out?"

"We did. Thanks," Jacob said.

"Just go to the kitchen when you get up, no rush. Maria will be happy to make you a late breakfast or early lunch—

depending on what time you get there. Dante and John are in his den working, and I think Quinn and I are going to go catch up with the others downtown. Call me when you're up and around."

"Thank you, Bella. For everything."

"I'll call you in a little while," Jacob said then hung up the phone, setting it on the nightstand before wrapping his arms around her.

With her head on his chest, she murmured, "I can't believe you're here. How did you know?"

"I may have been in cahoots with Bella and Reagan about the baby shower and bringing everyone here. My family should be here later this afternoon."

Taren lifted her head and smiled. "That's wonderful. I'm so glad our families are going to meet."

"Think you might want to get married while we have everyone here together?"

She bit her bottom lip. "Really? Tomorrow?"

"I was thinking tonight, but we could wait until tomorrow if that's what you want. I was just hoping when I spanked your ass tonight, instead of calling me Sir, you'd call me Husband."

She bit back a giggle. "No. Husband is for when you're making love to me. Sir is when I'm being punished."

He smiled and nodded. "Fair enough. So... what do you say? Will you marry me this weekend?"

Tears started streaming down her face as she nodded vigorously, squeaking out, "I would love to marry you."

He leaned over the edge of the bed and stretched his arm out, his fingertips grasping his grey pants, and he pulled them onto the bed to fish through the front pocket. Pulling out a black velvet box, he opened it so it was facing her. The oval shaped diamond had to be at least three carats and was set in a platinum band with a sparkling row of petite pavé diamonds.

"Oh my god," she whispered with her fingertips against her lips. "It's so beautiful."

Jake took the ring from the box and slid it on her finger. "Perfect fit."

Taren wiggled her fingers, admiring her engagement ring as it sparkled in the light, when a thought hit her.

"You just happened to have the ring in your pocket?"

He tugged her on top of him, tucking her hair behind her ear.

"Tinkerbell, you should have known I wouldn't leave you alone until my ring was on your finger. I told you, baby, I'm never letting you go again."

"Thank you for not giving up on me."

"Not a chance, my little fairy."

She studied his face a while longer before nuzzling into his chest, his arms instinctively tightening around her.

"I love you, Jacob Preston Smith. You're going to be a great dad."

"And husband," he murmured and kissed her hair.

She couldn't disagree.

Chapter Thirty-Seven

Taren

"What are you smiling about?" Bella asked as she sat down at the patio table with a fresh mimosa. Taren's family were on a new sightseeing tour while Jacob and Edward went to pick up Jacob's parents, his brother, Jack and Jack's kids.

"Just looking at my ring."

"Aw, you're so adorable. I miss the honeymoon phase."

"That is a beautiful ring. He has good taste," Reagan chimed in.

Quinn was noticeably silent, which was like chum in the water for the Jones sisters, who'd imbibed a few too many mimosas.

"So, Quinn. Are you ever going to come clean about what's happening between you and John?"

The dark haired woman, who was a few years their senior, just smiled and coyly remarked, "Come clean about what?"

"Ugh! One of these days, we'll get it out of you," Bella threatened.

Again, the woman only smiled.

"You really need to tell us," Reagan moaned.

Quinn's smile fell for a moment, then she finally said quietly, "There's really nothing to tell. He's been a good friend to me these past few years, that's all."

Bella's twisted mouth indicated she wasn't a believer.

"We're getting you drunk. Then you'll spill."

Just then, Dante and John stepped onto the patio, deep in conversation until they noticed the women. Taren curiously watched John as he immediately surveyed the group until his eyes landed on Quinn. He tried to catch her attention, which she appeared to avoid giving him.

"Hey, *mamacita!*" Bella said as she stood up. "We need to go into town and get your dress."

"What? A mumu?" Taren asked with a laugh.

"No. There's a silk dress I've seen in a little shop's window that will look perfect on you."

"Oh, I know exactly which one you're talking about!" Reagan added as they walked toward the house, past the men.

"Are you going, too, Quinn?" John asked as he touched her arm, his tone hopeful—like maybe she was staying behind.

Taren had gotten the impression when they talked about dress shopping that she hadn't been planning on coming with them, but changed her mind once he asked.

"I am."

"Oh, okay," the dark haired man said. "If you have a moment when you get back, I'd like to talk to you about some things. Maybe we could talk after dinner."

The beautiful woman's forced a smile. "Oh, yeah, sure. Of course."

Taren wanted to scream at John, "You idiot!" but chose to keep her mouth shut and looped her arm through Quinn's instead.

"Let's go into town!" she said cheerfully and grabbed the champagne bottle still in the ice bucket on their way inside. "I have a feeling you're going to need this," Taren whispered to her new friend as she handed it to her.

"I think you're right."

They all piled into the back of the black sedan, laughing and drinking from the bottle. Taren sighed and looked down at her water bottle.

"Aw, mommy, you'll be drinking with us again before you know it," Reagan laughed, wrapping her arm around her shoulder. "Now let's go find you a dress!"

*****

Jacob

He had to give props to the Jones sisters. Those girls were *good*. He'd had his doubts when Bella said to leave it to her, but she'd pulled it off—just like she said she would.

Looking around the big table in the Guzmans' dining room on the eve of his wedding, he sat back with his arm around Taren's chair, and watched their families interact as a wave of contentment washed over him.

There was laughter and smiles filling the room, with Bella and Reagan interjecting their own history into stories their parents were telling and Edward occasionally adding his own experiences with his brother.

Jacob hadn't realized how far back John and Dante's friendship went—the two were like brothers, having attended the same boarding school and then roomed together in New England while they attended different colleges in Boston.

Dante went to work in the family business after grad school, but it didn't take long for him to recruit John as his right hand man in the cartel. Now, they were attempting to slowly phase out of the Mexican mafia business and become legitimate. It was taking longer than Bella would have liked, Jacob knew that, but the two men's involvement with the cartel was becoming less and less. Dante had approached him again about becoming a partner in the near future, and he was seriously considering it.

Jake wanted to phase out of the mercenary business quickly and be done by the time the baby arrived.

It almost seemed like serendipity when Edward approached him later that evening on the patio about a job for his brother, Marcus.

"Funny you should mention that. Taren and I were just talking about me finding someone to take over my business. Have him call me in a few weeks after things have calmed down."

"Yeah, I definitely will."

Taren sidled up next to him and murmured in his ear. "I think something is going on with Jack and Rachel."

He looked around the pool area and at the table and chairs where the parents were and noticed Ashley coloring contently while Chase sat on Jacob's mom's lap. His brother, Jack, was nowhere to be found.

"What? Where are they?"

Taren gave a crooked grin. "Exactly."

"Don't let Bella or Reagan know. Holy shit, they'll be relentless with their ninja matchmaking."

"I think they're preoccupied with getting John and Quinn together, not to mention worrying about our wedding."

"How are we supposed to feel about Rachel and Jack hooking up?"

She shrugged. "They're adults. It's probably none of our business, but I did notice Rachel seemed to enjoy hanging out with Jack's kids today, so, maybe it's not a bad thing? We actually had just talked about the universe bringing her a family—maybe this is the universe's response."

"They live in two different states, Tink."

She answered with her usual woo-woo shit. "So? Let the universe deal with that."

He pulled her in his arms. "What does the universe think about us moving back to New Orleans?"

"I really don't want to start a new job knowing I'm going to be going on maternity leave in less than eight months."

"So, don't start one."

"I *like* working, Jake. It gives me purpose."

"What if you cut your hours to two days a week? At least until the baby comes, then you can decide if you want to work or not, and we can figure out where we want to live."

"So, does that mean you'll stay in Houston? With me?"

"Does it have to be at your apartment?" he teased. "Can we get somewhere bigger where I can have my own office?"

She let out a dramatic sigh, trying not to grin. "I guess, if we *have* to, but what do you need an office for if you're quitting? What are you going to do?"

"I don't know yet. Maybe nothing."

She snorted out loud, making him grin.

"What? I could do nothing. Being a dad will be my job."

"Just in all the time I've known you, you've always been working, spending countless hours in front of that computer. I have a hard time believing you could just be idle."

"Well, I have a few irons in the fire, should I decide I want to work. That's the beauty of it—if I *want* to. I don't *need* to work ever again. And neither do you."

"I want to work."

He shrugged. "Maybe you'll feel differently once the baby comes. Or when your ankles are so swollen that it hurts to be on your feet."

"You might have a point. I've seen pregnancy ankles in the ER—they weren't pretty. We'll see what happens."

"If you're only working a few days a week, maybe we can spend some more time in New Orleans?"

"Sure. You know I love New Orleans. Besides, I want to see your home."

"*Our* home," he corrected. "If you hate it, we can buy something else."

"I'm sure I'll love it." She paused. "Unless..."

"I have never brought a woman there, if that's what you were going to say."

"That's not what I was going to say."

That was totally what she was thinking.

He cocked his head. "No? What were you going to ask then?"

"Unless, um, it doesn't have enough bedrooms."

He smirked, "There's seven, not including my office."

"*Seven*! Why do you need seven bedrooms?"

"I don't—yet. But maybe we will."

"I'm not having seven kids, Jake."

"No, but if we have four they can each have their own room, then there's an office for you, leaving us with one guest bedroom."

"You mean you don't have a guest house on the property?" she teased.

He tried to school his expression when he answered, "I'd really consider it more of a pool house than a guest house..."

She shook her head and grumbled, "Rich people."

"You're one of us now." he whispered in her ear.

"What if we go to New Orleans next weekend?"

He shook his head. "Next weekend we're going to be in Bora Bora on our honeymoon." He was looking forward to French Polynesia and a little alone beach time with his bride.

She stifled a yawn, and he stood up, not caring that it was only seven thirty. She needed to go to bed early after he'd kept her up so late last night, and he still wanted some playtime before bedtime.

"We need to get you to bed, beautiful." In a lower voice, he added, "You have a punishment coming."

Her smile made his cock hard, and they started making the rounds of saying goodnight to everyone, citing the excitement had taken too much out of her, and she had a big day tomorrow—all true. When they reached Bella and Dante, the redhead wagged her finger at him.

"Uh uh. You're not welcome here tonight, Jacob. Sorry, you have to sleep at your villa—alone. It's bad luck to be together the night before the ceremony. The next time you see her will be when she's walking down the aisle."

"Nope." They'd been apart too long since the cruise—not to mention the goddamn seven years before the cruise, he wasn't spending another night away from her.

Taren turned to him and stroked his arm. "It's only one night, babe. We'll have the rest of our lives to sleep in the same bed. I don't want to tempt fate."

He stared down at her pleading eyes and felt his resolve dissipating. Glancing at Bella with a scowl, he snarled, "Fine," through gritted teeth.

"I will be checking the cameras. I'll know if you try to sneak in her room again, and I'm not above dragging you out by your ear."

He narrowed his eyes at her, but she only laughed.

"My house, my rules."

"Then we'll stay at my place."

"No, you won't," the redhead replied confidently.

His shoulders sagged because he knew she was right; no, they wouldn't. There was no use fighting her.

Glaring at Bella, he grabbed Taren's hand. "Come on, baby. Let's go make out in the corner, then. Away from the cameras."

Bella cackled as she called after them, "Keep your hands where I can see them!"

He would—Tink was right, they had the rest of their lives.

As he held her close to him, he put his hand on her belly and sighed. He'd have to be sure to include a thank you to the universe in his wedding vows tomorrow.

Epilogue

Taren

"How soon after the baby gets here can you fly again?" Jacob asked her as they got off the plane in Houston and she waddled to the car waiting for them on the tarmac. They'd been in San Diego visiting Bella and Dante so Jacob could finalize the paperwork for his interest in the dispensary business. That was going to be her last trip—her doctor said she couldn't fly after thirty-six weeks.

Their driver pulled up to the high rise they'd finally moved into. The private security guard in the front got out first then opened their door. The Sinaloans still hadn't caught the leader behind Madi's kidnapping, and with Taren's due date fast approaching, Jacob had become extra vigilant. There were two more guards in a car behind them who'd stand watch in the lobby and outside their front door.

She started reminiscing about her weekend with Bella.

"Dante and Jacob have banned me from interfering with John and Quinn, so I'm worried I'm going to lose my touch," Bella lamented one afternoon as they sat on the beach watching Madison play in the sand.

"*You* lose your touch? I find that hard to believe."

"Maybe I just read John and Quinn wrong," Bella said as she dug her toes in the sand. "I've been known to do that before—I didn't think Reagan and Edward should be together, and look at them. Those two are ridiculously in love.

Maybe John and Quinn are really just supposed to be the best of friends and nothing more."

"That might be one that just has to happen on its own," Taren offered as she let the sand run through her fingers.

"You might be right," the redhead said with a shrug. "Anyway, if anything is going to happen, they'll need to figure it out on their own. I'm officially minding my own business—at least as far as those two are concerned. For now. Dante wants to try and have another baby—I need to concentrate on distracting him from that."

"You don't want another one?"

"I'm thirty-eight. No, I don't want to get pregnant again. They're going to make me do all kinds of tests because I'd be considered high risk. Have you seen the size of the needle they use for an amniocentesis?" She shuddered. "No. Thank. You."

Taren laughed at her badass friend's fear of needles.

"Have you thought about adopting?"

"Yeah, but I'm not sure I want someone digging into my background too closely, you know? Since I'm supposed to be dead and all."

"Like mother, like daughter," Taren teased, then immediately clapped her hand over her mouth. "Was that in bad taste? It's not really something to joke about—I'm sorry."

Bella laughed. "I hadn't thought about it like that, but, that's pretty funny, actually. I hope Marcus gets that figured out soon. It's just going to get harder to disguise the fact that she's alive, the older she gets."

"You could always say you adopted her."

"We might have to. Are you going to go back to work once James is born?"

Running her hand over her stomach at the mention of their son's name, Taren couldn't help but smile. After some negotiation, they'd finally decided to call him James. "Maybe when he's three or four—and I'm sure it'd only be part-time. We travel too much for anything else."

"I understand that. I wish we could spend more time in Mexico, but Dante hasn't let Madi go back since Jacob found her in that warehouse. And he and I have only been back a handful of times since your wedding."

Taren smiled at the memory of that weekend. It truly had been magical. Bella and Reagan had done an amazing job, especially considering it had been so last minute—although not as last-minute as she'd originally thought. Jacob came clean on their honeymoon that in addition to working with the women on getting her to Mexico and talking to him, he'd planted that he wanted to marry her as soon as possible. The matchmaking ninjas' wheels started spinning in overdrive and were delighted when their plan came together, and they got to throw her not only an amazing baby shower, but an awesome wedding as well.

And she'd certainly enjoyed married life. Jake seemed to relish his role as husband and future-father and had spent every day making her feel loved and protected. However, the nights that she called him Sir had become nonexistent once she started her third trimester, and she'd been particularly bratty because of it.

"I'm keeping track, Tinkerbell," he'd warned in her ear. "Once James gets here, and the doctor gives you the okay, you're not going to be sitting down for a week. Maybe a month if you keep it up."

"Promises, promises," she snarked back.

"So brave," he'd murmured. "We'll see how brave you are in about five months."

Turns out, she regretted being so sassy.

****

Jacob

Being semi-retired at forty-one was pretty damn nice. It helped that his baby boy and wife kept him busy.

When Marcus had first come on board, Jacob made sure to play a role in any active case. Now, he was only doing that if it was a past client who had yet to work with Marcus. But Edward's little brother had been raring to go from the start and worked nonstop. Jacob didn't ask him what he was avoiding—he remembered those days seven years ago, when working was the only thing that kept him sane after breaking up with Taren.

The pot dispensaries were well-oiled machines. Dante, Bella, and John had perfected their business model, so opening a new shop was smooth sailing. They'd done a good job about divvying up each of the owner's involvement, so it didn't require much effort on any of their parts.

It also helped that Quinn was a master at making sure everyone did what they were supposed to. If Jacob were being honest, she was really the one running the show. They were lucky to have her. John better not fuck it up by getting involved with her and breaking her heart.

He and Dante had both voiced their concerns to John and were met with reassurances that, 'they were just really good friends'. Which, didn't seem to make Bella very happy, but she was overruled.

Tinkerbell was going to the doctor today. If Dr. Bonet gave the all-clear for them to be intimate again, he was whisking her away this weekend while leaving his parents in charge of James. They were in dire need of some sleep and sex—not necessarily in that order. And Taren had a red ass coming to her after all the sass she'd been dishing out these last few months. It'd only been in the last few weeks, as her 'all-clear' date loomed on the horizon, that she'd toned it down a notch.

It wasn't going to help her.

"I told you, baby. I'm keeping track," he'd said gruffly in her ear last weekend when she'd been impertinent, then tried to back-pedal—even calling him Sir when he'd simply smirked in return. He was counting the days.

But, he was also looking forward to sliding in between her thighs and fucking her slowly until she screamed his name. And falling asleep while still inside her. He'd really missed that.

Jake knew Taren missed sleep in general—she needed it a lot more than he did. While he'd been good about getting up in the middle of the night when James was fussy, seven times out of ten, the baby wanted to be fed—something Jacob couldn't provide.

"I know the feeling, buddy," he'd say wistfully and bring the wailing boy to suckle on his half-asleep wife's boob.

Taren was a great mom, and he wanted as many babies as she'd let him put in her.

"Don't even talk to me about another one until James's first birthday," she'd warned when he broached the subject.

Her incoming text was simply a smiling emoji, followed by: *All clear!*

Mountains or ocean?

Oh, mountains!

He grinned as his fingers flew. *My parents are all set to arrive tomorrow. Probably should eat a big meal tonight, get some extra padding on that ass. You're going to need it.*

The emoji she sent this time was a smiling purple devil. *Can't wait.*

Neither could he.

****

Go to www.BookHip.com/ZVZNVL to get a bonus epilogue about Taren and Jacob's naughty, mountain getaway!

What happens when Ramon Guzman, the head of the cartel, falls in love at first sight? With a nerdy, naïve American no less? He tricks her into marrying him, of course!

Get Flashpoint: https://tesssummersauthor.com/flashpoint

****

More in the Agents of Ensenada Series!

Read *Ignition*, the Prequel to Book One, Kennedy and Dante here:

https://tesssummersauthor.com/ignition-1

Read *Inferno*, Kennedy (Bella) and Dante's story here:

https://tesssummersauthor.com/inferno

Get *Combustion*, Reagan and Mason's story here:

https://tesssummersauthor.com/combustion-1

Thank you!

Thank you for reading *Reignited*! I hope you enjoyed Jacob and Taren's story as much as I did writing it. Would you mind leaving me a review on wherever you purchased this book (and Bookbub if it's not too much trouble)? Believe it or not, your review really does help get my book seen by other readers. xoxo

Appreciatively,

Tess

Flashpoint
Agents of Ensenada, Book 4

I always get what I want.

He's the ruthless patrón of the Guzman cartel... she's a nerdy, naïve software analyst, nursing a broken heart, poolside in Ensenada.

Their paths should have never crossed, but once they did, Ramon Guzman decided he's keeping his sweet American nerd. One way or another.

Even if that means he has to trick her into marrying him.

https://tesssummersauthor.com/flashpoint

Ignition
Agent of Ensenada, Prequel

Betrayal had always been part of the plan; falling in love complicated everything.

Dante Guzman

He knew within hours that Ruby Rhodes, the sexy little auburn-haired beauty, who just happened to sit next to him at his favorite bar and flirt with him all night long, was not who she appeared to be. Redheads were his kryptonite—everyone knew it, including his enemies who wanted to see the Guzman cartel destroyed. Just exactly who sent her and why was something he was going to have to figure out. At least playing along with her was enjoyable since part of her ruse seemed to entail sleeping with him and indulging his... let's say, *darker* desires.

Or maybe that wasn't supposed to be part of the plan, and she broke the rules.

Falling in love with Ruby was definitely not part of his plan, and Dante was going to have to punish her for making him do just that. Especially after he learns who she really is and why she was sent to seduce him.

Get it here: https://tesssummersauthor.com/ignition-1

Inferno
Agents of Ensenada, Book 1

Kennedy Jones

I'm a special agent with the CIA, and I'm good at what I do. In fact, I'm considered one of the best. I can play the role of anyone and eliminating bad guys without them seeing me coming is my forte—which is why I was chosen to take down the head of the Guzman family.

Dante Guzman is a ruthless, sexy, cold-hearted cartel money-man. And now it's my job to study him, learn his likes and dislikes—in and out of the bedroom—so I can gain his trust and access to his uncle, the head of the Ensenada cartel.

I just didn't count on falling into Dante's clutches.

Every second I spend with him he manages to pull me further and further into his world. And the more time I spend there, the deeper I slip into the darkness with him, the more I realize...

I like it.

Dante Guzman

Don't let my good manners fool you—I'm one cold-hearted SOB, and I control the family's monetary affairs with an iron fist. There's no place for weakness in my world. Show weakness, and you die. As simple as that.

So when a petite, feisty, hot-as-hell bombshell storms into my life, I didn't stop to think about the consequences of keeping her. I wanted her, and I always get what I want. Period.

Turns out, the stakes were too high...for the both of us. And there's going to be hell to pay if we're going to be together, to one form of the devil or another.

Get your copy of Inferno!

https://tesssummersauthor.com/inferno

Combustion

Agents of Ensenada, Book 2

She was meant to be mine—I knew it the moment we met. Too bad I'm about to kidnap her.

Mason Hughes

As a decorated CIA agent, I know better than to kidnap a former colleague's sister and hold her hostage on a ship in the middle of the ocean. The agency tends to frown on that sort of behavior. But desperate times call for desperate measures; I have my reasons, and they're good ones. I'll be forgiven with a slap to the wrist—at least for that part of the mission.

Until I tie Reagan Jones up and can't resist her when she presses her tight little body against mine. That's probably not so forgivable.

Then there's the issue of falling in love with her and refusing to let her go once the mission is over. Definitely not forgivable.

I have no idea what I'm thinking—we can't be together; it's not safe for her. I'm a spy, and she's a feisty art instructor from Fargo. Not exactly the perfect match.

Or is it?

Get your copy of Combustion here!

https://tesssummersauthor.com/combustion-1

Other Works by Tess Summers

Free Book!

The Playboy and the SWAT Princess

BookHip.com/SNGBXD Sign up here to receive my newsletter, and get SWAT Captain Craig Baxter's love story, exclusively for newsletter subscribers. You'll receive regular updates (but I won't bombard you with emails, I promise), and be the first to know about my works-in-progress.

She's a badass SWAT rookie, and he's a playboy SWAT captain… who's taming who?

Maddie Monroe

Three things you should not do when you're a rookie, and the only female on the SDPD SWAT Team… 1) Take your hazing personally, 2) Let them see you sweat, and 3) Fall for your captain.

Especially, when your captain is the biggest playboy on the entire police force.

I've managed to follow rules one and two with no problem, but the third one I'm having a little more trouble with. Every time he smiles that sinful smile or folds his muscular arms when explaining a new technique or walks through the station full of swagger…. All I can think about is how I'd like to give him my V-card, giftwrapped with a big red bow on it, which is such a bad idea because out of Rules One, Two, and Three, breaking the third one is a sure-fire way to get me kicked off the team and writing parking tickets for the rest of my career.

Apparently my heart—and other body parts—didn't get the memo.

Craig Baxter

The first time I noticed Maddie Monroe, she was wet and covered in soapy suds as she washed SWAT's armored truck as part of her hazing ritual. I've been hard for her ever since.

I can't sleep with a subordinate—it would be career suicide, and I've worked too damn hard to get where I am today. Come to think of it, so has she, and she'd probably have a lot more to lose.

So, nope, not messing around with Maddie Monroe. There are plenty of women for me to choose from who don't work for me.

Apparently my heart—and other body parts—didn't get the memo.

Can two hearts—and other body parts—overcome missed memos and find a way to be together without career-ending consequences?

Also available at TessSummersAuthor.com

San Diego Social Scene series

Operation Sex Kitten: (Ava and Travis)

https://tesssummersauthor.com/operation-sex-kitten

The General's Desire: (Brenna and Ron)

https://tesssummersauthor.com/the-generals-desire

Playing Dirty: (Cassie and Luke)

https://tesssummersauthor.com/playing-dirty

Cinderella and the Marine: (Cooper and Katie)

https://tesssummersauthor.com/cinderella-and-the-marine-1

The Heiress and the Mechanic: (Harper and Ben)

https://tesssummersauthor.com/heiress-%26-the-mechanic

Burning Her Resolve: (Grace and Ryan)

https://tesssummersauthor.com/burning-her-resolve-1

This Is It: (Paige and Grant)

https://tesssummersauthor.com/this-is-it-1

Sloane: (Ashley and Sloane)

https://tesssummersauthor.com/sloane

Boston's Elite series

Wicked Hot Silver Fox

https://tesssummersauthor.com/wicked-hot-silver-fox-1

Wicked Hot Doctor

https://tesssummersauthor.com/wicked-hot-doctor-1

Wicked Hot Medicine

https://tesssummersauthor.com/wicked-hot-medicine

Wicked Hot Baby Daddy

https://tesssummersauthor.com/wicked-hot-baby-daddy

Wicked Bad Decisions

https://tesssummersauthor.com/wicked-bad-decisions-1

Wicked Little Secret

https://tesssummersauthor.com/wicked-little-secret-1

Wicked Grumpy Heart Doc

https://tesssummersauthor.com/wicked-grumpy-heart-doc

Wicked Little Thief

https://tesssummersauthor.com/wicked-little-thief

About the Author

Tess Summers is a former businesswoman and teacher who always loved writing but never seemed to have time to sit down and write a short story, let alone a novel. Now battling MS, her life changed dramatically, and she has finally slowed down enough to start writing all the stories she's been wanting to tell, including the fun and sexy ones!

Married over thirty years with three grown children, Tess is a former dog foster mom who ended up failing and adopting them instead. She and her husband (and their six dogs) split their time between the desert of Arizona and the lakes of Michigan, so she's always in a climate that's not too hot and not too cold, but just right!

Contact Me!

Sign up for my newsletter: BookHip.com/SNGBXD
Email: TessSummersAuthor@yahoo.com
Visit my website: www.TessSummersAuthor.com
Facebook: http://facebook.com/TessSummersAuthor
My FB Group: Tess Summers Sizzling Playhouse
TikTok: https://www.tiktok.com/@tesssummersauthor
Instagram: https://www.instagram.com/tesssummers/
BookBub https://www.bookbub.com/profile/tess-summers
Goodreads - https://www.goodreads.com/TessSummers
Twitter: http://twitter.com/@mmmTess

www.ingramcontent.com/pod-product-compliance
Lightning Source LLC
Chambersburg PA
CBHW061117310726
48974CB00002B/573